MW00906446

Servalius Window

BY CLAUDIA WHITE

Servalius
Window

BY CLAUDIA WHITE

MP PUBLISHING

First edition published in 2015 by
MP Publishing Limited
Queens Promenade
12 Strathallan Crescent
Douglas, Isle of Man IM2 4NR British Isles
mppublishingusa.com

Copyright © Claudia White 2015
All rights reserved.

This book is sold subject to the condition that it shall not, by way of trade
or otherwise, be lent, resold, hired out, or otherwise circulated without the
publisher's prior consent in any form of binding or cover other than that in
which it is published and without a similar condition including this condition
being imposed on the subsequent purchaser.

The scanning, uploading and distribution of this book via the internet
or via any other means without the permission of the publisher is illegal
and punishable by law. Please purchase only authorized electronic editions
and do not participate in or encourage electronic piracy of copyrighted
materials.

White, Claudia.
Servalius window / Claudia White.
p. cm.
ISBN 978-1-84982-232-9
[1. Mythology, Chinese--Fiction. 2. Brothers and sisters --Fiction. 3.
Shapeshifting --Fiction. 4. Fantasy fiction.] I. Title.

PZ7.W582495 Se2015

[Fic] --dc23

Jacket Design by Alison Graihagh Crellin
Jacket Image by Larissa Kulik

ISBN-13: 978-1-84982-232-9
10 9 8 7 6 5 4 3 2 1

Also available in eBook

*This book is dedicated to
the wonderful village of
Warborough Oxfordshire, UK,
a place I still think of as home.*

Part
One

CHAPTER ONE

A dazzling shade of blue was the dominant color. Its cool depth soothed her; looking at it gave Anya a feeling of deep relaxation, as if she were floating through a brilliant sky. As the blue spread across the scene, its richness lightened, sparkling with shimmering, paler hues that merged into flamboyant greens, which faded in turn into vibrant, then creamy yellows. Around the edges, sunburnt-orange fingers forked through the surrounding landscape of warm grays and browns. A few bright splotches of white balanced the scene.

Anya Harding smiled as she studied her latest painting. "I'll call you *Renewal*," she breathed.

When she finished admiring her work, Anya covered the canvas with an ancient golden velvet cloth—the ceremonial drape that had been used in all her family's artistic unveilings over the last millennia. She smiled to herself again, as if enjoying a private joke.

She placed the painting at the center of her large gallery, which usually held a number of Harding family paintings.

Today it was emptied of all but this latest work. Tonight was the annual spring unveiling. On the first day of each season, the family of Harding celebrated with a new masterpiece. It was a tradition that had stood as long as the Harding clan itself.

Anya stepped out into the garden. The glow of the coppery sunshine had arrived in perfect Servalian time. She loved the changes of season, each ideally timed to satisfy the expectations of the centuries. Servalius was a place where people never needed to discuss the weather—it would be as it always was. She breathed deeply as she took in the beauty of her garden. Though they lacked the rich colors she preferred in her art, the coolness of the plants pleased her; pale-colored flowers grew in neat groups, pleasing to the eye and soothing to the senses. It was the epitome of an orderly Servalian landscape, and a dramatic contrast to the energy on her canvas.

The realization that the sun had dipped beneath the horizon took Anya by surprise. She had no idea how long she'd been enjoying her garden—no idea what the time was or where it had disappeared. "That's the first time I've ever done that," she said to a pale yellow flower at her elbow. "If I don't hurry, it'll be the first time a Harding has ever missed their own showing. That would never do—especially for tonight's program."

Through the schoolroom window, Mia Prowst watched the light fade into a dusky sky. Her classmates and teachers had left ages ago; no one seemed to notice she'd stayed behind. It was the first day of spring, and the first day of her journey into adulthood. She sat motionless at her empty desk, trying to figure out where it had all gone wrong. She was a Prowst and should have marched easily into this part of life's journey, as her family had done for generations. But apparently nothing was going to be that straightforward.

Mia's childhood had been perfect—though really, all the children on Servalius could say the same. Servalian children were born with the knowledge of mathematics, language, literacy, and the basics of science already etched into their brains. Children didn't attend school until the beginning of maturity, after their twelfth birthdays. Until then, Servalian children only had to be children. And they all did that very well. Children never rushed into adulthood—it arrived soon enough. After all, there were no preparations to be made; there was nothing to worry about, no confusion to work through. Things happened when they happened and that was that.

When they entered school, they were ready. School was easy. There were no books. There were no exams, no homework assignments, quizzes, or papers to fill their hours. There were no tests to assess achievement because achievement was guaranteed. Servalian children knew from birth what they would be when they grew up—the same as all the members of their family, because children were always born into the right family. A banker was always born into a banker's family, a carpenter into a carpenter's, a musician into a musician's.

Everything was already planned out. In school, teachers needed only lecture and students listen and learn. The children's brains were like sponges, absorbing and retaining everything they'd need for their future.

On this fine and perfect spring day, Mia Prowst entered school the same as everyone else. Because she was a Prowst, she attended all the lectures designed to further her education in chemistry. All Prowsts from the beginning of time had been chemists.

But unlike the rest of her classmates, Mia's first day had been difficult—actually, impossible! She hadn't understood anything in her lectures. She had almost fallen asleep during organic chemistry. Even now, long after her classes had ended, poor Mia sat stunned, as if frozen in her seat. No one knew about her situation—no one could have understood. While all the other students sat mesmerized by the lecture, Mia was confused and miserable. All Prowsts had achieved the highest standard in their fields. How could it be that she couldn't seem to grasp even the simplest concept of her destined profession?

Mia turned far enough to stare out the classroom window. The half disc of the sun was now sitting on the horizon. "I've got to get out of here," she whispered to the silent room. "It'll be better tomorrow. I was probably nervous—I always get nervous…even though I'm not supposed to." There were no books or papers to gather up, and Mia ran quickly out of the school building, her arms wrapped around herself.

Outside, processions of people were already making their way to the Harding Gallery. All the ladies were dressed in gleaming white ceremonial robes, their long hair braided and twisted into intricate styles piled high on top of their heads, only fitting for the occasion. The men, in similar robes of gray, wore their hair in single plaits down their backs.

Mia looked down at her beige school uniform, not at all appropriate for the evening's event. Her long curly blond hair hung loosely. She wished she'd brought her robes along to school, but this morning she hadn't felt any need. She should have known. In Mia's life, there was always something—always some divergence in an unchanging and unchangeable society.

She ran along the central pathway, through the neat rows of plants in the city gardens. Her house was just on the other side of the gardens, but if she ran quickly—

"Mia!" Her mother's calm voice rang out from the other side of the hedge. "Where have you been? You're late, and we've got to keep our place."

Mia walked over to her waiting family, her stomach in knots. Her mother, father, and brother looked at her with only the slightest unease. Her mother smiled weakly.

"You're not dressed," she said in the same measured tone, eyeing Mia's uniform, "but that can't be helped. We cannot risk losing our place. You'll have to come as you are."

Reluctantly, Mia joined the procession. She might have explained about her day at school and asked for understanding, maybe even asked for help, but she had no idea how to do that. And she knew no one would understand how to help her even if she did.

CHAPTER TWO

The procession into the Harding Gallery was slow and stately. Anya Harding smiled warmly, greeting the hundreds of guests as each family took their place around the stage— places their families had occupied for generations. The final rays of sunlight shimmered through the tall, curved windows set into the walls, providing the only light in the gallery. Then, as one, the entire audience silently sat down.

With the sun lost below the horizon, the silvery threads of the three Servalian moons took over. All color vanished as the white light illuminated the room in shimmering tones. Anya Harding stepped forward into a beam of brilliant moonshine, her tall frame and black hair bathed in the moon's glow. "Welcome!" she greeted warmly. "Tonight's festivities are focused on a single thought: renewal. Servalius is glorious and perfect. There is no need for change. We live according to ancient doctrines to achieve a perfectly balanced life…a perfectly planned path. Life any other way is unthinkable. Perfection is our plan, our desire, and the only way we know. But there is always need for renewal, and that is our theme this evening."

Anya basked in the glory of the moment. There was no screech of chairs moving, no guests coughing or fidgeting, no babies crying, nor any other suggestion that she was surrounded by hundreds of other souls. She didn't need to hear them; she could feel their presence. The gallery rippled with anticipation.

"We will begin with a very special symphony created by Alfred Canat. In a moment you will all experience the sensations offered by this wonderful piece of music."

Anya motioned to a tall silver-haired man standing alone in the far end of the gallery. The light that seemed to flow from her hand illuminated Alfred Canat. He gave an elegant bow to his hostess and then moved forward purposefully to stand beside her at center stage.

Mia Prowst was spellbound. She wasn't alone; everyone in the audience was holding their breath, just as they always did at a Harding Showing. Her stomach tightened in anticipation, and she watched with awe as the strong form of Alfred Canat took his position. His arms rose evenly and slowly, then hovered for an instant in midair. When he brought them down again, the music began—not in the air, only in the minds of the guests in the gallery. Mia melted into the sound as it pushed all thoughts away. She felt content and invigorated all at once.

Anya studied with pleasure the contentment on the faces of her guests. The music was communicating where words fell short. Calm passages were followed by intense sounds that built to tremendous falls. At the highest point in the melody, Anya unveiled her masterpiece. She pulled the ceremonial drape away from the painting just as the music hit its crescendo and brilliant blasts of light streamed in through all the windows at once. All eyes focused on the astounding colors and ethereal textures of Anya Harding's *Renewal*. The canvas exploded with vitality and movement that only the Family of Harding artists were able to create.

No one questioned the surreal spectacle of the canvas. There was not a front or a back; there wasn't a side or an obstructed view. It didn't matter where people were in the gallery—everyone was in the perfect seat. The transformation from flat canvas to a globe of artistic achievement was all part of the Harding phenomenon.

The music continued to play in their minds, complementing the magic of the art in front of them. As each member of the audience enjoyed the sight and sounds, each in turn felt the strength of their own rejuvenation.

Especially Mia Prowst. Her difficult day dissolved completely. For Mia had experienced an extraordinary renewal—a renewal so incredible as to be unthinkable for any Servalian.

CHAPTER THREE

Mia was the first to leave school for the twenty-third day in a row. She walked briskly, looking down at her feet as she hurried through the gardens of the City Park, her curly golden hair blowing around her head like a mass of sparkling serpents. She took no notice of the neat rows of flowers bordering the path or the meticulously trimmed trees lining her route. She didn't see people playing, walking, or riding bikes. For the last few weeks, she left school every day in the same distracted yet sunny mood. She didn't even notice the first Baffleball games of the season starting to crop up in the city parks.

Baffleball was a very popular sport, played in warm weather months on any grassy field big enough to hold the players. Servalians of all ages leapt at the chance to grab the oval ball, dribble it wildly, and run at top speed to the goal. There were no teams—it accommodated anywhere from two to two hundred players, and everyone played for him or herself, and it was more like organized mayhem than a game as everyone ran, jumped, dived, and spun trying to intercept the ricocheting ball. It was Mia's favorite activity, but recently she had no time for it.

Consumed with her own thoughts, Mia skirted the inside of the Baffleball field. At the same time, equally oblivious to Mia, the entire field of players moved rapidly into her. It was lucky for her that this was a relatively small match of ten, as even ten people, when they are piled on top of you, can feel like a hundred. Calmly, Mia requested that the mound on top of her promptly remove itself—a request that didn't have to be made, since the game was still on. As quickly as they'd crunched into Mia, the players disentangled themselves and were off again as if nothing had happened.

Adam Garvin was the only one to stay behind. He was about halfway under the pile-up, and once untangled he helped Mia to her feet. Adam was two years older than Mia and had been her best friend all her life—and, until recently, her closest companion. The two had rarely skipped a day together since they'd met as toddlers.

"Thank you," Mia said simply as she brushed the grass and dirt from her school uniform. She looked up at Adam, who stood six inches taller than her; his ginger hair was blowing into his eyes, his mouth set with its characteristic smile, ready to hear her explanation as to where she'd been over the past few weeks. Abruptly, she announced, "I'm going to be an artist."

If any other person had made this announcement, especially in such a matter-of-fact way, it might have given him pause. But this was Mia. Adam studied his lifelong friend:

her pretty face staring up at him, her green-blue eyes open wide, sheltered from the sun by his shadow. An innocent and determined expression was firmly etched on her face, making her appear older than her twelve years. Calmly, he replied, "An artist?"

"Hmmm," she said absently, looking away. "Like Anya Harding."

"Anya Harding!" he shrieked, overtaken by surprise. Adam was accustomed to Mia's strange ways, her fleeting fancies and her fantastic imagination, but this was really too much. "Mia, what are you talking about? You can't be a Harding artist—you weren't born a Harding, you were born a Prowst!"

Mia looked past Adam toward the Harding Gallery. "I don't feel like a Prowst. I don't even *look* like a Prowst. The members of the Prowst family are always tall and dark— dark complexion, dark hair, dark eyes. Look at me!" She threw up her hands, the gesture making her blond curls flail.

"That's true, but not everyone looks like their family. Look at me." Adam was the only ginger- haired Garvin.

"And you said you thought maybe you were different from them, too…admit it! You said sometimes you think you were born wrong."

"That was a long time ago. I don't feel like that anymore. I'm managing my studies and looking forward to my future as a…banker," Adam said, though he couldn't help a slight hesitation. "Mia, you can't change your destiny. It's simply not done. How can you learn something you're not born to do?"

"That's just it. I know I wasn't born to be a chemist…I *was* born wrong. And I know what I feel: I was meant to paint. I can see how to do it; when I look at things I know I could put them on paper. Since the Showing, I've been testing my skills. But before I tell my family, I must see Anya. I know she'll teach me."

Adam screwed up his face. "But she's not a teacher—she wouldn't know how. I don't know what will happen if you start asking these kinds of questions…what will people do when they hear such nonsense?"

"I'm going to ask her anyway. That's where I'm going… to the Harding Gallery."

"I'll come with you," Adam insisted, determined to ease her away from this insanity.

Mia hadn't been back to the gallery since the Showing. No longer emptied of artwork, the main gallery was beautifully decorated with hundreds of Harding masterpieces. The sight took Mia's breath away. Every image danced with vibrant colors and shimmering movement. Mia and Adam walked around the massive room, both in awe of the enormity of the Harding collection.

"Mia," Adam said in a whisper, "shouldn't you find Anya?" He was surprised at himself; he wanted to discourage Mia from this embarrassment, but something prodded him to hurry her along.

"I'm going to, I just want to make sure…I really want to do this. It's the only thing I've thought about since the Showing. I've never thought of chemistry this way. This must be my true course, but I don't know how to create these paintings. It's not like seeing something real and recording it on paper. I don't know if I could ever do this." Mia's voice dropped with her spirits. All her plans were evaporating as she realized that the Harding artistic genius was more than talent; it was like magic.

Mia walked from wall to wall, the paintings showing brilliantly in the natural light from the windows. She stopped, took a deep breath, and turned to face the center of the room. The stage was still in place, and Mia relived the memory of the Showing. The light from the windows changed with the lateness of the hour and streams of sunshine raced into the room, concentrating on the stage. Mia couldn't resist its pull. She walked to the stage, followed silently by Adam. The memory of the magic of the Showing became their sole focus, an unspoken connection between them as the memory of the music of "Renewal" penetrated their minds.

Silent, awed, they stood just at the edge of the stage; only two steps up would put them in that thrilling spot of light that brought Anya Harding's paintings to life. The music and light was as powerful as they had been weeks ago, and Mia and Adam were drawn into its energy, almost unconsciously climbing the steps to the stage. Mia found her voice at last.

"Look, the painting is back. I didn't see it at first, but it's still here." The two were so absorbed in the dramatic colors and movement of the painting that they didn't notice that they were no longer alone.

"Are you sure this is necessary?" Alfred Canat asked emotionlessly from the far end of the room, too quietly for Mia and Adam to hear.

"It's the only way," Anya Harding replied, her voice equally bland. Neither she nor Alfred said anything else as the light gradually faded into thick dusk. Then in an instant the light dissolved completely, along with Mia, Adam, and the painting itself.

Part Two

Chapter Four

Indigo's eyes quivered under tightly closed lids, pools of teardrops massed at her lashes. Her cat, Aunt Phoebe, leaned in toward Indigo's slightly opened mouth, her whiskered face tickling as she drew closer. It was just what Indigo needed to draw her back to consciousness. Her huge dark eyes opened slowly and a smile crept across her face. "Good morning, Auntie," she cooed, patting the sleek calico fur of her companion. "Thanks for waking me. I had that stupid dream again."

For as long as Indigo could remember, she had a horrifying recurring dream of falling. She could never remember where she had fallen from or where her drop was taking her. All she remembered was the music that penetrated her mind during the descent. The melody was intoxicating, communicating something that she could never quite grasp, a perfect counterpoint to the colors swirling around her. It was always the same—exciting yet terrifying. As frightening as the sensation was during the nightmare, she always awoke feeling exceptionally refreshed, with the images from the dream quickly fading away.

Indigo propped herself up on her elbows and surveyed her domain. She happily lived alone in a one-room flat with a bed, toilet, sink, tiny fridge, and hotplate—not much to some, but looking around gave Indigo a sense of pride. She was only fourteen years old and successfully provided for her home with very little outside help. Most of her possessions were items discarded into skips by people who obviously had more than they needed. Some had been broken, ripped, or bent when she found them, in a state that would discourage most people. But Indigo was not like most people; she had a wonderful imagination, and after she repaired, straightened, and polished her acquisitions, they looked quite trendy. She had collected a myriad of broken dishes and glued them together to form the most unusual patterns, and even had an old tarnished lamp that she had polished to a brilliant shine and fashioned a fabulous shade for out of plastic bottles.

Throwing back the patchwork quilt made from bits and bobs of fabric she had sewn together into a magnificent cover, she crossed to the window to estimate the hour, as she didn't have a clock. "Auntie, it looks like you woke me up just in time." Indigo hurriedly dressed in one of her many chic creations—this one a mini skirt of denim from someone's discarded trousers and a loose blouse made out of old chintz curtain material. She admired her reflection in the window, considering her tall, sleek posture, shiny, straight auburn hair, and silky, tanned complexion. After a cuddle with Aunt Phoebe, she gathered her writing supplies and books and left for school.

Indigo had lived in Paris all her life…at least, it was the only place she could remember living. Of course, she hadn't always lived alone. Not that she had lived with her parents…she could never remember doing that. In fact, she didn't know anything about who they were or might have been, or even if she had any brothers or sisters. But when she was very young, she had lived with a kind old lady named Phoebe. Indigo didn't know how it came to be that they lived together, but that didn't matter to her at all because the years they lived together were very happy.

Sadly, Phoebe had disappeared the day before Indigo turned twelve. She seemed to have vanished without reason, without a trace, and without consequence with the exception of leaving Indigo alone. Aside from Indigo, no one cared because Phoebe had always kept to herself. The police didn't do anything except fill out a missing person report. It was all very disconcerting. So Indigo just kept living in the flat and hoped Aunt Phoebe would return someday.

At first Indigo was filled with questions about what had happened to Phoebe: Did she run away with a traveling show? Did she meet the man of her dreams and escape to some island of paradise? Or was she traveling in space on some fantastic adventure? But the longer Phoebe was gone, the less Indigo indulged in suppositions. After all, she was very capable of looking after herself—and she did it with style. Plus, she had a feeling deep in her heart that Phoebe was happy wherever she was.

Indigo was a strong believer in silver linings and blessings, and this belief had paid off time and time again. For instance, on the day of Phoebe's disappearance, a very small kitten arrived. It seemed only fitting to honour the old lady who had been so kind to her. From that day on, if anyone asked, Indigo could honestly say she lived with her Aunt Phoebe. Of course, Aunt Phoebe didn't get out much and was unable to attend any functions, meetings, or other get-togethers. And since Indigo did such a splendid job of taking care of herself, nobody was concerned in the least or had any reason to ask difficult questions.

Indigo Jasper was not totally without means. She had a bank account. It was more like a trust fund she'd been told some distant relative had established for her. She had never met this relative; in fact, she didn't even know what kind of relative it was—grandparent, uncle, cousin? She often wondered if this person existed at all, as they never tried to get in touch with her and the bank didn't have any more information. All she knew was that the money was intended for her education, and that was precisely how she used it.

Another of Indigo's blessings was that Paris was the home to one of the finest science schools in the world. What luck for her to live in the neighborhood of the Horace Stumpworthy School for Science Excellence! Ever since she was very small, Indigo had known she would attend this particular school, though the opportunity was extended to very few students each year. But nothing dissuaded Indigo from her dreams, and she studied hard for the entrance exam.

After receiving her results, Indigo and her Aunt Phoebe (who unfortunately could not attend) were invited to meet with the famous Horace Stumpworthy himself—a privilege extended to very few students. "My dear," he crowed, shaking her hand warmly, "your paper has earned a nearly perfect score! Only one other student has marks even close to yours. I would be most pleased if you would attend our school." And so she did.

That had been over a year ago. Every day since then, Indigo left the small, ornate building that housed her flat, walked around the corner and past the intoxicating aromas from *la patisserie* that always caused rumbles in her stomach, and then all but skipped down the elegant tree-lined avenue that led to the school. She walked with brisk, determined elegance and a pleasant grin, not quite a smile, but certainly not a frown.

This day, however, was a little bit different. As she strutted down the avenue with the brilliant spring sunshine warming her back, she whispered, "*Níg-ge-na-da a-ba in-da-di nam-ti ì-ù-tu*" three times before her grin waned almost imperceptibly and her breathing increased ever so slightly. "Oy, Anu," she sighed. "I understand the words, but what does it mean?"

CHAPTER FIVE

As she did every morning, Madame Rousseau marched purposefully into the classroom. Placing her books on the lectern at the head of the class and pausing only a second to adjust her glasses, she launched into the day's subject. Madame Rousseau was a general science teacher, crossing the boundaries of biology, chemistry, physics, and earth science. She was a very small woman with a shock of gray hair that stood on end most of the time, a somewhat grayish tone to her skin, and small blue-gray eyes that stared out through her narrow black spectacles. What she lacked in beauty and warmth of personality, she made up for in a flamboyant teaching style that Indigo adored. She had a way of bringing to life obscure pieces of information and entertaining her students with fascinating facts rather than dull statistics.

Today's lecture was on the Scientific Revolution during the Renaissance. *I love this stuff*, Indigo thought as she readied her notepad.

Madame Rousseau paced the floor in front of the students. "Many of our current scientific methodologies have their roots in this fantastic time in history. The telescope was invented to help explain the nature of our solar system and Earth's place in the universe. Clocks were first developed, as well as the first microscopes. In mathematics, calculus was invented, and many Early Renaissance machines were the basis for modern machinery that came centuries later. Although medicine didn't make much progress until the next century, we can assume that the Scientific Revolution paved the way. It was a time of great discovery, and, strangely, a time of many bizarre and sacred superstitions, such as…"

Indigo enjoyed the study of history and its relationship to the present and to the future. But as she listened intently to Madame Rousseau, her concentration began to wane and her mind to wander—something that, until recently, had never happened. Suddenly, there were times when she had difficulty knowing what was real—like now, as her sight blurred, the classroom strangely dark and murky around her. She began to cough uncontrollably, gasping for breath as the air seemed to swirl with thick smoke.

Indigo turned and ran from the room. Sweat burst from her pores, saturating her clothing. The smoke billowed around her, choking her with every breath. It wasn't only the smoke—the stench was incredible, the smell of… "Not again!" she cried when she realized what she was seeing. Horrorstruck, she watched three women's bodies being consumed by fire. A crowd of people had gathered—some cried, some cheered. Their pitiful cries silenced, the putrefied air was the only reminder of the women's fate. Indigo felt faint, retching as she pushed through the mass of people. One voice droned persistently above the sounds of the crowd—*a priest*, she thought.

It wasn't her first witch-burning, and the way things were going it wouldn't be her last. She loathed the concept, the cruel farce called justice. Only fear forced her attendance. If anyone knew the truth about her, she might find herself viewing the scene from the other side of the flames.

She stumbled through the crowd, away from the scene... but that voice, that single voice followed her. Had they discovered her secret fear? Her panic erupted as she heard the voice clearly, close by—

"Indigo! Indigo Jasper!"

She shuddered, shaking her head to rattle her brain back to consciousness. Adrenaline racing, she found it difficult to focus on who was after her.

The scene in front of her was clearer now. The heat was gone and the air was cool. Clear sunshine streamed in through the classroom windows. Fifteen pairs of eyes were staring at her.

"Felix, please take Indigo for some fresh air. She looks ill," Madame Rousseau said curtly.

In the next instant, Indigo was stumbling out of their lesson, helped by her classmate, Felix Hutton. "I'm really okay. I feel fine," Indigo protested.

"You look like you're gonna puke!" Felix replied, putting his arm around her waist for support.

"I can walk," she said softly, not trying to push away.

"You look terrible…you're all white, actually kinda green. What happened?" Felix asked.

Indigo shook her head. "I don't know. One minute I was listening to Madame Rousseau, and the next everyone was staring at me." She stopped midway down the hallway, rubbing her face to restore her natural color.

Felix's eyes widened. "What's that thing on your neck? It's all oozy and red."

"What are you talking about? I don't have anything on my neck," Indigo said, trying to maintain an air of calm though her expression was somewhat panicked.

"Yes, you do! It looks like a burn," Felix insisted.

Clutching her neck, Indigo hurried to the nearest girls' bathroom and reluctantly stood before the mirror, shoulders hunched, head ducked in turtle fashion. She squinted at her image, hesitating a moment before carefully removing her hand. Felix was right. There was a horrific sore on her neck, complete with oozing blisters and peeling skin. It looked like a serious burn, but she couldn't feel anything; there wasn't even a hint of pain.

She didn't panic—in fact, quite the opposite. Her lips twisted in disgust as her head rolled back, aiming a determined glare at the ceiling. "I can't believe this is happening. What next!"

Only a few minutes had gone by but Felix was ready to send in a search party. His mind raced. *She isn't well…she's probably lying on the floor, calling out for help…I have to go in.* He summoned his courage and pushed the door open, but it stopped abruptly, a shrill cry erupting from the other side.

"What are you doing?" Indigo barked, holding her nose where the door had bashed into her.

"You were in there for ages. What's happening?" Felix asked, his voice shaking. He peered around her arm, somewhat obscuring her neck as she massaged her nose. There was no sign of the horrible gaping sore. His eyes shot to hers, then to her neck, and back again. "Where's the…ah…where did it go? What was it?"

"Oh, that," she answered casually. "I sometimes get these weird rashes when I'm nervous. First time I've ever had one that bad…but as you can see, it's gone now." She leaned toward him, turning her head so that her neck was clearly visible. "Now let's get lunch. I'm starving."

Felix couldn't believe what he'd seen—or more to the point, what he hadn't. Dazed, he followed Indigo to the school café.

As with everything in Horace Stumpworthy's world, the Science School's café was sumptuous and elegant. Students and faculty dined in the lushness of a garden located on the third floor of the school. It looked more like a trendy restaurant than a school cafeteria, refreshing the minds, bodies, and spirits of those who entered—all part of the ostentatious world Professor Horace Stumpworthy had created. Felix often surprised himself with the realization that not everything the man had done was bad.

For Felix, it was nothing new, as he'd been living in Stumpworthy's mansion since arriving in Paris with his family more than a year earlier. He had grown accustomed to Horace's world. His parents Jake and Elaine Hutton, his sister Melinda, Professor James Mulligan, Dr. Harmony Melpot, and her uncle, Joe Whiltshire—the people he considered his family—were the only ones who knew the truth about the great Horace Stumpworthy: his evil plans and his unexpected disappearance. No one else needed to know because, since Stumpworthy's demise, nothing had really changed. Things were still managed according to his plans, with Professor James Mulligan running the school, along with Harmony, who administered the science education program. Stumpworthy himself was even seen occasionally—with a little help from Felix, who could transform into his likeness. No one knew the truth, and that was how it would remain.

It wasn't unusual for Indigo and Felix to have lunch together. They had only been friends a short time, but it seemed longer to Felix. Their connection was brilliant. During their first lunch, they had discussed the miraculous properties of traveling slime molds and the intrinsic values of spore fungus. Who could have asked for a better start to a friendship?

Today might have offered another appetizing discussion, but Felix was absorbed by Indigo's earlier condition. "What happened to you?"

"Nothing. I don't know what the fuss was all about," Indigo chirped.

"Nothing?" Felix's tone was incredulous.

"I tend to be a little sensitive to things like witch-burning…all that talk about women being roasted alive." Indigo shrugged, stuffing a huge piece of lettuce into her mouth.

Felix frowned. "Madame Rousseau didn't say anything about women being burned alive. She only noted it was strange that during the Scientific Revolution in the 17th century, when some of the basis for modern scientific theory was born, people were still very superstitious and still practiced witch-burning in parts of the world."

"What can I say? I have a very active imagination. There are some things that really freak me out, that's all."

"Are you sure you're okay?" Felix asked slowly.

Indigo smiled sweetly. "Felix Hutton! I didn't know you cared," she said, batting her eyes at him.

Felix flushed a not entirely handsome shade of ripe tomato. "Never mind. I just thought…never mind." He looked down at his unfinished lunch, but his appetite had evaporated.

After a minute of uncomfortable silence, Indigo plunged into a topic she knew interested Felix tremendously. "What did you think about Monsieur Hillcot's explanation of fractals? I thought I understood them before, but he's mucked up the whole thing for me," she said, waving her hand in the air.

It worked. Felix was almost as fond of fractals as he was protective toward his favorite math teacher. As defense poured out in between mouthfuls of food, Indigo sat back, trying hard not to laugh. She wasn't going to let him know she actually agreed with him.

At the end of the day, Felix rode home with Dr. Harmony Melpot, his biology teacher as well as his family friend and housemate. "How's Indigo? I'd heard she wasn't feeling well," Harmony remarked.

"Says she's fine," Felix said, "claims nothing was wrong with her." He thought about dropping the subject, but this was Harmony, a person he'd always been able to talk to. In contrast, most of his classmates were intimidated by Dr. Harmony Melpot, which might have owed to the fact that she glided into a room like the Greek Goddess Aphrodite— she was just a little too perfect to be real. Her tall physique and chiseled features could turn heads wherever she went. More likely, it was her direct manner that was a little off- putting. Her penetrating gaze left many feeling as if they had just had their innermost secrets exposed and their very soul closely inspected.

Felix continued, "There was this weird thing...after we left the classroom, she had a horrible...ah...*thing* on her neck, like a serious burn. Then it went away...*it just went away!*"

"What was it?"

"She said she gets rashes sometimes when she thinks uncomfortable thoughts, but I can't believe it was just a rash. It was oozing and red, really painful looking...one minute it was there, then it was gone," he said in amazement.

"Is she concerned?"

"That's another thing! She said it was absolutely nothing, she's not worried about it at all," he snorted.

"Then I don't think we need to be, either. Look, if there was nothing there after a few minutes, she was probably suffering an unusual psychosomatic reaction to something. If she has it under control, that's the best anyone can do." They both fell silent for a long time. "She's a smart girl, that one—really grasps science and mathematics. She'll give you a run for your money," Harmony said with a smirk.

Felix jumped, wondering if Harmony had perfected the art of reading minds. He *had* been thinking a lot about Indigo…thoughts he would rather nobody else knew about. Felix looked up to see if Harmony was teasing him. She wasn't smiling anymore; a scowl had replaced her relaxed and happy demeanor. Even if she *could* read thoughts, she wasn't bothering to now—she'd entered the driving zone, adopting the tense, maniacal posture of drivers in Paris rush-hour traffic.

Felix slumped comfortably into his seat, returning to his private thoughts. He turned away from the traffic that was at a standstill in front of them, catching sight of his reflection in the side mirror: a tall, thin, average-looking geek of a boy, glasses slipping down his thin nose as usual. He didn't allow his thoughts to stray back to the fantasy of Indigo…she was his friend, and sadly that would be the total sum of it.

CHAPTER SIX

Thoughts about Indigo were pushed aside as Felix and Harmony drove through the gates of the Stumpworthy estate. It wasn't the grandeur of the palatial home, with its immaculate gardens and grand façade, that pulled Felix's mind away from his friend; after all, this extraordinary classic French stone mansion had been his home for more than a year. Nor was it the massive quantity of homework in physics and math that distracted him, though he was eager to tackle that difficult calculus equation that had evaded him all day. It wasn't even the fact that tonight was the televised finale of the European Chess Championship—an event Felix had looked forward to all year—which dominated his thoughts. As they drove up the long stone driveway, Felix was thinking about something far more distracting and infinitely more disconcerting: Melinda, his twelve-year old sister.

Melinda was in many respects Felix's opposite. In contrast to Felix's tall, thin body, Melinda was short with rounded features—not fat, just nicely full. Felix's thin features, narrow, dark eyes, and bushy dark hair contrasted with Melinda's circular face with big blue eyes set as islands in a sea of freckles, her head crowned with an abundance of unruly reddish-brown hair.

Where Felix was conventional, Melinda was daring, her exceptionally active imagination making her life one big adventure. Before discovering that they were Athenites—a race of people with the ability to transform into animals, other people, or even to disappear completely—Felix and Melinda had little to do with one another. And although Felix at first despised the idea of morphing into anything, whereas Melinda immediately relished the thought of exploring her powers of transformation, this unusual fact of life had ultimately brought them closer. Of course, Felix still rejected the thought of growing fur, paws, fangs, or antlers: he used only a few of his talents, such as disappearing or taking on someone else's appearance, and of course telepathy had proved an exciting attribute when it developed. Melinda, on the other hand, took advantage of all of her talents—sometimes, quite unfortunately, attempting everything all at once, with strange and complicated consequences.

Felix flinched as the car pulled to a stop just opposite the front entrance, and he looked out at the twelve marble steps that led up to the ornately carved front doors. The sun was still shining brightly, highlighting the vibrant colors of the pink and purple bougainvillea and showing off the huge white blossoms of the hibiscus that bloomed elegantly in massive stone pots bordering each step. There were no other signs of life. Felix smirked, shaking his head when he thought about what might be lurking on the other side of those doors: a giant squid with Melinda's beaver-like smile, perhaps?

"What do you think she's done today?" he asked Harmony.

Harmony smiled for the first time since leaving the school. "Melinda?"

Felix nodded. "Let's see," he chirped. "Yesterday, she was completely faceless…"

"Now that was eerie…you could see where her face was meant to be, because her hair was floating all around the space—thank goodness for that, or she would have been totally headless." Harmony shuddered.

"The day before," Felix went on, "she had Clydesdale hooves instead of feet. And remember last week—the feathers?"

"How could I forget?" Harmony laughed. "She was covered in them!"

"That was brilliant! She decided to go out for a little flight, but forgot to transform the rest of her body into a bird, so her human body was completely covered in feathers!"

"In all fairness, she wasn't completely human. She did have a beak." Harmony frowned. "You know, that could have been dangerous if she'd tried to fly out of an upstairs window."

Felix didn't even try to subdue his laughter. "I'll never forget it. There she was, running around the garden flapping her arms and hopping into the air…a weirdo in a feather suit! She had no idea that she was still human and couldn't figure out why she wasn't flying!"

Harmony covered her mouth in a weak attempt to hold back her chuckle. "Come on, Felix—she's trying to control herself, but an adolescent Athenite can experience strange changes when their mind wanders."

"Which, in her case, is all the time! I'm going through the same changes, but you don't see me growing antlers, and certainly not feathers." He scoffed.

"But remember the first time you changed into the spitting image of Professor Horace Stumpworthy? You nearly gave James Mulligan a heart attack."

Felix rolled his head back on the seat, smiling at the memory. "He got over it, and I learned to do something that has come in pretty handy over the last few months. We've been living rather well since we have access to Stumpworthy's bank account."

Harmony nodded. "True enough. And Melinda's transformations have saved the day on a few occasions as well." Felix shrugged as Harmony added, "It's just a matter of control. Need I remind you about *your* first accidental attempt at vanishing? You were invisible for more than a week."

Felix sighed. "Look, I'm not criticizing. I'm actually looking forward to seeing what she's morphed into today. Consider it the perk of living with a lunatic." Before Harmony could respond, he opened the car door and slid out, leaning back in to finish, "I just don't like the big surprises—like the time she greeted us as a twelve-foot alligator." Harmony's eyes widened and she nodded. Felix winked. "Today I'm prepared…I'm going to find her before she finds me." He shut the car door and then bounded up the stairs.

Felix crept in through the front doors, closing them silently behind him. The house was unsettlingly still. His father, Jake, was away on an assignment with an International Health Organization and his mother, Elaine, had mentioned that she would be locked away in her office on the third floor all day—something about finishing an article that was due on her editor's desk the next morning. Joe Whiltshire, Harmony's uncle, was also out of town, as he often was these days, this time on an archeological dig in South America. James Mulligan had stayed behind at the Science School, where he was required to attend some meeting or other, and Harmony was locking the car. That accounted for all the members of the household except Melinda.

Everything was dreadfully quiet. Felix knew that could only mean one of two things: his sister wasn't home, or she was in some form that wouldn't make a lot of noise— perhaps a bat or, heaven forbid, another rendition of some winding, twisting snake. Felix closed his eyes, trying to zero in on any telepathic activity in the house. It didn't take long to locate something, and he smiled to himself: she was in the library.

Scrambling his thoughts to evade detection, Felix skirted the foyer. He slipped past the enormous and imposing sculpture of the god Bes, with its lion head and human body, and then rounded the eight-foot-tall statue of the Minotaur that stood sentry at the base of the stairs. The house was filled with this kind of artwork; there were gigantic figures of ancient gods and paintings of fabled half-man, half-animal beings in almost every room. Not that long ago, Felix had hated them, reminders of an ancestry he rejected. After he accepted his heritage, these amazing artifacts only served as a reminder of the man who had collected them: Professor Horace Stumpworthy.

Felix didn't often conjure up images of the professor, but sometimes, like now, they simply slipped in. Stumpworthy had been one of the most influential scientific minds of the day. He was world renowned in more than one field of expertise; he was fabulously rich and very powerful, and had been Felix's hero—until, of course, Stumpworthy's evil side crept into the picture. On more than one occasion, the professor had tried to eliminate the Huttons and their friends...Felix shook off the uncomfortable images. There was no sense thinking about the late Horace Stumpworthy now.

Felix scuttled on tiptoe down the hallway toward the library. His sense of Melinda's presence strengthened with each step. He reached the library but didn't enter yet. "She's probably ready to pounce—I just know it," he giggled to himself. "Unless I can surprise her first."

He leaned back against the wall, trying to calm the flutter in his stomach. No sounds came from inside the room, but he knew she must be in there. He rested on his shoulder for an instant before peering in for a glimpse of whatever mischief he felt certain Melinda must be preparing.

Felix felt a jarring disappointment when he saw only a small, dark-haired human head, resting on the back of the nearest of the three sofas that circled the massive fireplace dominating the library's first floor. His eyes darted around the rest of the three-story room, scanning the walls of bookcases for any sign of a more interesting creature. There was nothing. *I'd have preferred the giant squid*, he thought as he walked into the room, his eyes focused on the person resting comfortably on the sofa. There were no horns or donkey ears or feathers or scales...it was simply a human head.

"Hi, Mel," he hailed casually.

She didn't answer, swiveling around instead, after which Felix's mood lightened considerably. He stared in awe at the petite, wrinkled-faced Chinese man looking back at him over oval-shaped spectacles balanced near the tip of his nose.

Felix was momentarily torn: he was pleased that his sister had attempted something, but he wasn't sure he liked the idea of her transforming into a human image. Up until that moment, he had been the only member of his family to accomplish that kind of transformation. He shrugged at the inevitability of her accomplishment. "What are you supposed to be, Chairman Mao?"

She didn't answer, nor did her bemused expression change. Felix glided over to the far corner of the room and deposited his schoolwork on a desk. "Well, if you are supposed to be Mao Zedong, you didn't quite make it. Mao wore his hair cut short, not in a long plait like yours. You look more like some ancient wise man," he quipped as he set to work organizing his books and papers. "You know, Mel," he added helpfully, "when you change into someone else, you really have to know a lot about them. What on Earth possessed you to become some old, wrinkly Chinese guy? Wait a minute...of course. You're studying Chinese history, aren't you? You must have transfo—"

"Felix!" Melinda barked, cutting into his speech—but the sound didn't come from the man sitting on the sofa.

Felix jerked toward the doorway, where Melinda stood frozen in place, her face screwed up in a look of anguished embarrassment. "I see you've met Dr. Li Zhang, my Chinese history tutor," she squeaked, nodding in the direction of the man who was still watching Felix over the top of his spectacles.

Felix's normally pale complexion drained to a whitish gray. His knees buckled, causing him to lunge forward as a burning, acidic sensation migrated out of his stomach up into his throat. He turned and smiled sickly at Dr. Zhang. "I'm pleased to meet you," he croaked formally. "If you'll excuse me, I have...ah...something important to see about in the...ah...another room," he stuttered, brushing past Melinda in his hurried exodus.

Dr. Zhang returned his attention to the small book he held on his lap as if nothing had happened. "Melinda, were you able to find the book on Chinese stories you wanted to show me?"

Melinda stared nervously at her teacher for a second, then shook her head before taking her seat on the sofa directly across from him.

Without moving his head, Dr. Zhang looked over his glasses at his pupil. "Maybe you can locate the book before our next lesson. In any case, I have brought this one for you to study. It is called *Book of a Thousand Proverbs*, and it is an excellent beginning for your study of Chinese history."

Melinda nodded. "Mum says that a lot of history is disguised in old stories."

Dr. Zhang nodded. "That is very true, but do not confuse proverbs with fables. Proverbs are adages used to explain situations and concepts. They can be modern in origin, like *it takes two to tango*, or ancient, like *gu zhang nan ming*: clapping with one hand produces no sound. In this case, whether the modern or ancient version is used, they mean exactly the same thing: it sometimes takes two people to create or solve a problem. Since we are studying Chinese history, we will study only Chinese proverbs, but they are used all over the world. This book contains sayings written more than two thousand years ago concerning significant moments in Chinese history, and they are still used to describe human behavior today."

Melinda grimaced. She had hoped to study Chinese fables—folktales about how people transformed into animals. Stories that described her own Athenite heritage.

Dr. Zhang noticed her expression and smiled. "I think you will enjoy this approach to history…a subject I believe is essential in knowing what the future may bring. You see, the study of ancient civilizations shows us where we have been, but since history repeats itself, it may also allow us to see a bit about our future. It can be argued that our lives and beliefs have advanced over time. Technology has brought advancements in medicine, transportation, entertainment, and knowledge that could never have been conceived centuries ago. We have even learned to understand and accept other cultures though education. Having said that, I believe people are the same, with the same desires that were present many millennia ago. You may be surprised at how familiar the observations of the ancient Chinese seem in relation to our modern society."

"Are you saying things really don't ever change?" Melinda eyed him suspiciously.

Dr. Zhang looked thoughtfully into her eyes. "There was a proverb written more than two thousand years ago: 'Watching the tree to catch a hare.'" Dr. Zhang smiled warmly. "Which means, the only thing that does not change is that everything changes."

CHAPTER SEVEN

Felix stared at Indigo as she shoved an entire quarter of her sandwich into her mouth. "What are you looking at?" she barked, swallowing the last bits of bread.

Felix's mouth dropped open. He had been staring intensely at her, trying in vain to read her thoughts. "Ah... sorry...I was, um...I mean, I must have been lost in thought."

"What were you thinking about that made you look all bug-eyed?" Indigo persisted.

A high-pitched giggle escaped as Felix nervously adjusted his glasses, which, as usual, were slipping down his nose. He said the first thing that came to mind. "China."

"China," Indigo repeated.

Felix shrugged, diverting his attention to his own half-eaten sandwich.

"What about China?" Indigo pressed.

Felix didn't look up from his sandwich as his mind raced to come up with an answer. He shivered remembering the beady little eyes of Dr. Zhang staring at him over his stupid spectacles. He thought about his sister's diatribe at breakfast that morning…how she did drone on. Unfortunately, he had been successful in tuning out her incessant yapping about her lesson from the day before. He moved his gaze to the floor, and then shot up straight as something clicked in his memory. "FEET!" he yelped.

Indigo curled her lips. "Feet? You were thinking about Chinese feet?"

He grappled with the one bit of information Melinda had been able to plant in his brain. "It's a proverb: Binding your feet…"

Indigo cut in. "…to prevent your own progress."

"That's it!" Felix chirped excitedly, then looked down at his hands clasped on the table. "Yes, that's it." He nodded coolly, trying to save face.

Indigo got a faraway look in her eyes and began rambling much the same way Melinda had at breakfast that morning. "It was written a few hundred years before the birth of Christ—well over two thousand years ago. It was used to describe how this one Chinese ruler—the King of Qin who ruled in the third century BC—was kicking all the non-Qin scholars out of the country. He thought that would benefit his people, but what happened was the reverse. His country suffered, while the countries where the scholars went prospered."

Felix assumed that nodding would be an appropriate response.

"In Chinese it's pronounced *guo zu bu qian*," she said in perfect Mandarin. She picked up her pen and notebook and scribbled four elegant Chinese characters. "This is how it's written…there is only one written Chinese language, but loads of spoken dialects."

Felix rocked back in his chair. "Do you speak Chinese?" he croaked incredulously.

The glazed look in Indigo's eyes dissolved. She took a deep breath, then shrugged, glancing unenthusiastically at her half-eaten sandwich. "I'm not really hungry anymore," she said, sliding the plate toward Felix. "You can have the rest if you want. I've got to get going," she announced, pushing away from the table.

"Oh…ah…okay." Felix stood up. "Do you still want to meet in the library later?"

She shook her head, fumbling with her notebook and book bag while absently mumbling, "*Níg-ge-na-da a-ba in-da-di nam-ti ì-ù-tu.*" Felix blinked at her.

"Sorry? Is that Chinese?

Indigo didn't answer. Then, without another glance at Felix, she pivoted and hurried from the room.

"Let me know if you want to work on our biology project this weekend!" Felix called fruitlessly after her. He frowned at her retreating back. "Girls," he groaned as he sat down and pulled her unfinished sandwich over.

Indigo marched down the hallway, never lifting her gaze from the floor, quietly repeating, "*Níg-ge-na-da a-ba in-da-di nam-ti ì-ù-tu*" over and over. As soon as she had exited the building, her pace looked more like a bewildered shuffle. "What is happening to me?" she whispered. "I don't speak Chinese! That is…I didn't yesterday, but I sure do today." She snorted in disbelief. "How and when did I learn Mandarin? And where did all this knowledge about Chinese history come from? I've never studied it in my life!" She picked up her pace; her breath was coming in short gasps. She rounded the corner, following the route that would take her back to her flat when she stopped and slumped against the wall of *la patisserie*, whose tantalizing aromas failed for once to distract her away from her quandary.

A few seconds passed before Indigo's confused grimace melted away. She pushed off from the wall; her posture was again strong, and her confident expression had returned.

"So now I'm an expert on Chinese history. Not only that but I can speak and write Chinese," she said proudly. "I don't know how it happened, or why, but there's no denying that it. Why be upset? I should be celebrating. It's a gift, that's all…a weird, unexplainable blessing of knowledge," she decided cautiously.

She turned and walked steadily back toward the school, whispering, "*Níg-ge-na-da a-ba in-da-di nam-ti ì-ù-tú*" until the corners of her mouth twitched into a smile. A slightly bemused expression swept across her face, but it only lasted an instant before she smiled and nodded smugly to herself. "I think I'm beginning to understand."

CHAPTER EIGHT

It was eleven o'clock Saturday morning, and Melinda's boredom had reached the level of agony. She had been staring out her bedroom window for what seemed like hours, watching as the torrent of rain beat against the glass. She clenched her fists at the downpour. There was no end in sight; the sky was dark in every direction.

Elaine Hutton glided by Melinda's bedroom, her long violet dressing gown fluttering elegantly in the draft created by her long stride. She paused in the hall, then retraced her steps and looked in at her daughter. "Melinda, instead of staring out the window and making yourself miserable, why don't you join me for swim?"

"Maybe later," Melinda groaned without looking at her mother.

Elaine walked over and placed a hand on Melinda's shoulder. "Don't you realize how lucky we are? We live in a grand house complete with its own indoor swimming pool and gym. Just because the weather has upset our plans doesn't mean the day has to be miserable." Elaine flashed her green eyes while pulling her mane of silky red hair into a ponytail. "Come on—let's have a great day together in our own tropical paradise."

Melinda's broody expression lightened a fraction. The spa only two floors below, with its huge swimming pool tiled intricately in the image of a mermaid, did seem rather inviting. She eyed her mother curiously. "Can I transform into something?"

Elaine narrowed her eyes. "Like what?' she asked suspiciously.

"I don't know…maybe some kind of water creature?"

"NO ANACONDAS!" Elaine snapped. "I still shiver when I think about the last time you did that…a five-meter snake floating in the pool!"

Melinda looked only a little guilty. "I didn't hurt anything. And besides, I wasn't thinking about becoming a snake today," she added innocently.

Elaine raised one eyebrow. "No crocodiles, alligators, piranhas…in fact, no predators of any kind!"

"What difference does it make if I'm a predator? I'm not going to eat anyone." Melinda turned her attention back to the deluge of wind and water pouring from the sky. "I really wanted to go to the grand opening of the Chinese Garden today," she sighed, "but the rain has ruined everything. There were going to be dragon dancers and music and a special tea ceremony."

Elaine smiled. "It's only been postponed." She patted the top of Melinda's head, catching her fingers in a tangle of curls. She turned to leave, calling back over her shoulder, "Why don't you see if Felix is up for a swim? He was studying in the library last I saw him."

Felix was hunched over the desk in the library, writing furiously. He hadn't looked up from the stacks of textbooks that surrounded him in hours—until he heard the *thwack... thwack...thwack* sound in the hallway. "What is she doing now?" he sighed, looking for Melinda through the empty doorway. When she didn't appear, he turned his attention back to his work.

Thwack...thwack...THWACK...THWACK... The sound was coming closer. Felix cringed but tried to ignore his annoyance.

THWACK...THWACK...THWACK.

"MELINDA! Whatever you're doing, knock it off! I'm trying to study!" He glanced at the door again, rewarded this time by the sight of his smiling sister. "I thought you were going out," he sniffed.

Melinda smiled. "If you ever looked up from your books you would know that it's raining buckets outside."

"So?"

"So they have postponed the festival." She looked proudly down at the feet. "I'm going swimming."

Felix followed her gaze to the floor, where he saw two shiny black seal-like flippers where her feet should have been. "I don't believe it," he hissed.

"I wasn't really in the mood to transform completely. I'm curious to see if having my own flippers is better than wearing scuba fins. You should try this—it feels wild."

Felix smiled, shaking his head as Melinda waddled across the marble floor and fell backward onto a sofa, kicking her flippers into the air. "It should feel wild...or at least weird," he laughed, "but I think I'll let you tell me all about it. It's not my kind of thing, if you know what I mean."

Melinda giggled. "I know. You only like the boring stuff."

Felix's face contorted into a devilish grin. *She thinks she's so clever*, he thought. *I'll bet I can still make her pulse race.* He closed his eyes and froze his movements, then almost instantly transformed into the image of Professor Horace Stumpworthy.

James Mulligan trundled from the dining room down the hallway into the foyer, wiping bits of dried eggs and droplets of coffee out of his droopy gray mustache. He panted as he neared the front door, exhausted from the exertion—something that his bulky body saw little of these days. The bell rang again.

"I'm coming, I'm coming," he grumbled. "I'm not the butler, you know." He pulled open the massive front door. "Oh, my dear...do come in out of that infernal rain! You must be soaked through."

"Thank you, Professor." Indigo smiled as she dripped into the house.

"Now, to what good fortune do we owe this delightful visit?" The silver-haired professor smiled, still plucking bits of his breakfast out of his whiskers.

"BES!" Indigo yelped as she struggled out of her soggy, no-longer-waterproof raincoat, then pulled off her waterlogged boots, exposing her intricately darned, multicolored, and very wet socks. "The Egyptian god who protects mothers and children."

"That's right, but I'm not sure I understand why you..." Mulligan paused, taking her coat gingerly with his thumb and index finger and holding it at arm's length to avoid the dribbles of water splashing onto the floor. "Let me hang this up for you—won't be a moment, the closet is just down the hall." He shuffled through the foyer, leaving Indigo to examine the massive statue in the center of the room. When he returned, she looked quite at home as she twirled around the room admiring paintings and sculptures of fabled creatures.

"I feel like I'm in a museum," she said, smiling.

Mulligan's full jowls vibrated slightly. "The study of mythology has always been a favorite around here."

Indigo frowned. "I love all this stuff. They..." She held up her hand, gesturing to the artwork, "...represent some of my favorite stories. They're almost like old friends," she finished, looking dreamily around.

Mulligan coughed, feeling heat rise to his cheeks. "Yes, yes...*old* friends. I feel the same way. But you didn't come here just to see the artwork, did you?"

Indigo giggled. "You're right, I didn't. I was actually on my way to a Chinese Garden celebration, but it was cancelled due to the weather. I thought I'd see if Felix might like to work on our biology project. I hope he won't mind that I came by without calling first."

"My dear, if he minds then he is a fool. I'm sure your visit will be very welcome. And if I'm correct, I can lead you right to him…he's usually studying in the library. Let's go and surprise him, shall we?"

CHAPTER NINE

Professor Mulligan and Indigo had only taken two steps down the hallway when Melinda's scream echoed. A second later, Felix gave a sinister laugh.

The professor's forehead beaded with perspiration. With a quiver in his voice, he sighed, "As I expected, Felix is in the library...as is Melinda. Have you met her—that is, have you met Felix's sister?" he asked haltingly.

Indigo shook her head. "It sounds like I'm about to," she chuckled, glancing up at the professor. He didn't look at her, instead fixing his gaze straight ahead. Indigo cleared her throat. "Felix has only mentioned a few things about her. She sounds...ah...lively."

Without looking at her, Mulligan laughed nervously. "Indeed she is. Unusual imagination...a bit of a dreamer... very unlike her brother." He raised his bushy gray eyebrows, glancing at Indigo. "She doesn't know that I know about her nickname for me; she calls me Professor Walrus," he sighed, shaking his head. "Don't ask me why—I haven't the foggiest idea where that came from."

Indigo swallowed a smile, noticing for the first time that the professor's full, flabby jowls, along with his large drooping gray mustache and matching eyebrows, did lend a walrus quality to his appearance. For a startling instant she imagined enormous tusks jutting from the corners of his mouth.

Mulligan turned his attention back to the hallway and the library at the end of it. He took a step but then stopped abruptly; the not-too-distant memory of Melinda's face on the head of a lizard unnerved him. His watery eyes popped open as wide as the folds of his skin would allow and he commanded in a most un-Mulligan-like manner, "You wait here—I'll let them know that we have a visitor." He trundled off as fast as he could, huffing and puffing from the effort.

He was still in the hallway, peering into the library when the sight of Horace Stumpworthy gawking at him from across the room made his knees wobble. But it was the image of Melinda's flippers that almost made him faint. He fell forward, grabbing hold of the wall. "Quickly," he hissed, "Indigo is…"

"Professor, are you all right?" Indigo gasped, running up behind him.

"INDIGO!" Felix's voice yelped out of Stumpworthy's mouth as Melinda flipped backward over the sofa, falling into a heap on the floor. She jumped to her flipper-encased feet, smiling awkwardly as she met Indigo's eyes. Felix straightened to assume Professor Horace Stumpworthy's full six-foot two-inch height and opened his mouth as if to speak, closing it again before a sound escaped. Nobody said a word.

Seconds began to feel like hours. Sweat trickled down the back of Felix's neck as every eye seemed to be focused on him…that is, on Professor Stumpworthy. *HELLO! JUST SAY HELLO*, his mind screamed, but he couldn't unclamp his jaw to force any words out. He glanced at Melinda, then at Mulligan, both with *Say something, stupid* written on their faces. His shirt was sticking to his very wet back.

Indigo smiled; her cheeks flashed pink and she looked away nervously. She met Melinda's eyes, only for an instant, and then took a quick visual tour of the library's circular construction, unbelievable number of books, splendid ornamentation, and floor-to-ceiling dome-shaped windows that let in an incredible amount of light, even though the day outside remained dull and dreary. Within seconds her eyes were back on Felix, or rather Stumpworthy. "Your library is magnificent," she said, cringing when her voice cracked into a giggle. "I'm sorry, I don't know what's got into me," she said, trying to suppress her laughter. "I mean, it's just that you've surprised me…what I mean is, I've never seen you dressed casually before."

A high-pitched squeak escaped Stumpworthy's lips as Felix's thoughts went wild. *Stumpworthy always dresses in suits and formal stuff, not in my jeans that just happen to be three inches too short for him! And he wouldn't be caught dead wearing a red t-shirt with SCIENTISTS DO IT WITH MOLECULES emblazoned across his chest!*

Professor Mulligan cleared his throat and shakily stepped into the room. "Sorry to bother you, Horace—I thought I'd heard Felix in here," he said, struggling to keep his voice level. "Indigo has come by as a bit of a surprise so they can work on their biology project together. Perhaps we should go back to the foyer until we can locate him," he added to Indigo.

"Felix was here a minute ago," Melinda giggled. "You just missed him! I'm sure he'll be back in a second, if you want to wait."

Felix slowed his breathing to regain his composure, fighting the urge to throw something as his sister. "It might be best to wait in the foyer while Melinda goes in search of him," he said in a perfect Horace Stumpworthy voice. He turned to face Melinda, who was finding it difficult to suppress her laughter. "Melinda, if you've sorted out that problem you were having earlier," he said, glancing down at her feet, "could you please go up the back stairs to Felix's room and let him know that he has a guest?" He turned back to face Indigo. "Melinda is our little helper around here... she may not be as clever as her big brother, but she is full of fun, aren't you, dear?"

Melinda glared at him and then glanced down at the floor. She closed her eyes for an instant and willed her flippers to return to human feet. Then she smiled coyly at her brother, deciding to have a little fun at his expense, and began walking around the sofa, slapping her feet down on the marble floor to make the loudest *thwacking* sound she could manage.

Felix's eyes bulged and he hurried around the desk, placed a hand on Indigo's back and guiding her toward the doorway. "In the meantime, perhaps Professor Mulligan can show you some of the…ah…*my* artwork along the way."

Indigo looked slightly confused, but she didn't say a word and allowed herself to be guided out of the library. As she and Mulligan vanished up the hall toward the foyer, Felix spun around to face his sister, who had now collapsed on the sofa and was kicking her bare feet into the air. She was laughing so hard she had to muffle the sound by holding a pillow over her mouth. Felix was tempted to give her a hand.

"It's not that funny," he muttered, rolling his eyes.

"Oh, but it is, *Professor*," Melinda howled, pointing at his ironic T-shirt. "You better hurry up—and don't forget to change!"

As the rain trickled to an end, the exhausted clouds opened under the first steely rays of moonlight. The front garden glistened in gray and silver hues as the dusk gave way to the colorless darkness of the hour. Felix watched through the front door as Harmony drove down the driveway, taking Indigo home. He closed the door, leaning back against it as it shut. Glancing down at his watch, he noted the hour for the first time since Indigo had arrived earlier. After the uncomfortable scene in the library when she had first arrived, everything else had gone as normally as could be expected. They had spent the entire day working on their biology project together. He sighed happily; it had been a very long day, but a very nice one.

He shuffled back down the hall into the library, where Melinda was waiting for him. "I need to talk to you," she announced. "I have to tell you that Indigo is a bit weird."

"Coming from you, that may just be a compliment," Felix seethed as he walked over to his desk and began fumbling with some papers.

Melinda sighed loudly, shaking her head in frustration. "Felix! What I'm trying to tell you is that when I looked into her eyes...well, I could see that she wasn't an Athenite..." She paused as Felix jerked around to face her. "...but she's not human, either."

CHAPTER TEN

"You heard me. She's not human," Melinda insisted as deep furrows dug their way across Felix's forehead. He stared at her for only a second before shaking his head in disgust.

"Indigo *is* human; you, however, are deeply disturbed," he seethed through clenched teeth.

Melinda ignored him. "Both times when our eyes met, I saw something I've never seen before," she said, pacing the length of the sofa. "Human eyes reflect who they are; Athenite eyes reflect animal images. Indigo's eyes…" She paused as if she didn't know what to say next.

Felix already knew all about Melinda's ability to tell the difference between humans and Athenites by looking into their eyes. It was a rare talent sometimes called *Ch'ing-Wa Sheng*, named after the Chinese frog spirit for vision and understanding. What he didn't understand was what it had to do with Indigo, and he was rapidly losing his patience. "*What about Indigo's eyes?*" he barked.

Melinda met his gaze. "There was nothing there at first. It was like I was looking down a tunnel with nothing at the end. It was eerie. But when I looked the next time, I saw people— lots of people. It was like I was watching a hundred movies all at once, except these people weren't like reflections, they were like…ghosts," she finished quietly, watching her brother, who was opening and closing his mouth, not making a sound but looking very much like a tuna out of water. "Felix, did you hear me? I said they looked like ghosts, and that's just not normal." Melinda hesitated, then smiled. "Well, maybe it is normal for her, whatever she is."

On the third floor of the mansion, Elaine Hutton was hard at work in her office. She had been writing about a mythological creature that she could prove was not the product of someone's imagination. Her work in mythological history had taken her all around the world. The author of about a dozen books on the subject, she was recognized as an expert in her field: a champion of the misunderstood; a proponent for protection and rights for the previously fabled.

Felix entered the office unnoticed. The light from the computer screen cast an eerie greenish glow, a fitting backdrop for Felix's mood. Occasionally a loose board would squeak under the pressure of his weight, but his mother didn't look up. His eyes adjusted to the darkness and he glanced around the room that had once been a servant's bedroom. Three walls were lined with shelves crammed full of books, magazines, manuscripts, family pictures, and miniatures of some of the same mythological statues found throughout the house.

Elaine's desk was dwarfed by the piles of books and papers stacked on top; her computer was barely visible, nestled in the center. She sat with a straight back, never so much as glancing down at her fingers as they found each letter on the keyboard with incredible speed. Her long red hair had been pulled into a ragged bun, secured in place at the back of her head with two pencils. Wisps of straggling locks fell around her face.

Without warning, Elaine looked up and smiled. "Ah, Felix," she said, stretching, "I didn't hear you come in. What brings you up here?"

"What type of creature might reflect ghosts in their eyes?" he asked hastily.

She rocked back in her chair. "That's an odd question for you...you've never shown the slightest interest in this subject. What's up?"

"Melinda *thinks* she saw the reflections of ghosts in Indigo's eyes," he said sheepishly.

Elaine stood up, rolling her stiff shoulders. "Well, let's see." She walked over to the bookshelves and pulled out a thick green volume. She thumbed through the book, stopping about midway. "I suppose Hades, the Lord of the Dead, and maybe his dog Cerberus." She paused. "Yes, of course Cerberus." She looked over at Felix. "Cerberus was charged with guarding the Underworld...he had three heads so, although nothing has been written about it, I suppose at least two of his eyes must have reflected the images of those he was meant to guard."

Felix shook his head. "I'm quite certain that Indigo is not a three-headed dog, and I'm almost positive that she's not Hades in drag," he drawled.

Elaine laughed. "Of course not. I'm just trying to think of what, or who, might fit the description." She handed Felix the book and pulled out another. "Here we go," she said as she scanned the contents. "The three Fates: Clotho, Lachesis, and Atropos. Since they decided how long a mortal would live, I should think their eyes would be full of ghostly images." She handed this book to Felix as well and retrieved three more. "There's also a fairy from Ireland—I can't remember her name, but it was said her eyes reflected *our* souls and hearts, and of course pixies and Altheia, the fairy of revelation."

Felix shook his head again. "Talking about fairytale creatures isn't helping."

Elaine pulled several more books off the shelves. "Remember that many myths, fables, and fairytales were written to disguise reality. It wasn't that long ago, historically speaking, that people were labeled as witches because they were different. All sorts of stories circulated about the magical powers of these so-called witches." She stopped for a minute and looked up, smiling at Felix. "Remember that colony of Singeliis we met on that Greek island?"

Felix shivered involuntarily. The memory of coming upon at least a dozen one-eyed naked giants frolicking on the beach was *not* one of his favorite holiday recollections.

"I'll admit, it was a bit frightening to see them at first, but they turned out to be lovely people; very kind and giving." Elaine smiled. "It's hard to imagine that centuries ago people called them *Cyclops* and said they were murderous monsters: eating men alive, biting off their heads, then using the bones to pick their teeth. All nonsense, especially when you learn that Singeliis are vegetarians!"

She turned away from her bookshelves and looked into Felix's eyes.

"This isn't helping, is it?" When Felix shook his head, she sighed, folded her arms and stared at her desk with an unseeing gaze. "You know," she spoke the words softly, "we may not have Melinda's ability to see into the soul of another, but we all have the ability to see beyond the color of someone's eyes. Right now I can tell you're worried and frustrated about someone you care about."

Felix's milky complexion burnt crimson as he searched for something to refute her statement, but he remained silent.

Elaine smiled knowingly. "I don't know enough about what Melinda can or cannot see to help much; this is still a very new area to me. All I can say is that whatever Melinda saw is probably not as new or unique as it might first appear. There are so many incredible beings in the world, some with qualities that may seem too extraordinary for us to accept as normal." She looked at the stack of books cradled in Felix's arms and smiled. "The answer to your friend Indigo's ghosts might be right at your fingertips."

Felix's arms ached by the time he reached the library. Carrying down all fifteen volumes in one go had seemed an efficient idea when he had left his mother's office. But as he wobbled down the sweeping staircase, the books seemed to have doubled in weight, and by the time he entered the library, they felt as if they had tripled. His arms shook under the strain and his fingers had gone numb, so that when he reached the large square table that sat in front of the three sofas, directly in front of the fireplace, his muscles gave out completely and he dropped all the books at once.

"HEY," Melinda shrieked as one bounced off the table and hit her in the side of the head. She had been sitting cross-legged on the floor, using the table as a desk while reading a book of her own.

Felix didn't seem to notice her as he picked up one of the books and began flipping through the pages. "There may be something about the Three Fates, or that dog, the one with three heads," he said with authority. He looked up and stared blankly across the room, then groaned. "This is stupid! Now I'm not making any more sense than Mum...or you."

Melinda looked up as Felix furiously flipped through the pages. "Felix, you should read this book," she said, but Felix only shrugged, clearly not listening. She stood up, careful not to lose her place, and then she shoved her book on top of the one in Felix's hands. "Read this," she commanded.

Without looking up, he began reading. Absently he walked over to the nearest sofa and collapsed onto it, never taking his eyes from the print on the page. Several minutes passed before his eyes lifted, a bemused smirk replacing his scowl. He looked at his sister as if only just noticing she was in the room. "This is too weird," he wheezed, rolling his head to rest on the back of the sofa.

"I know, but it definitely matches what I saw," Melinda began, but Felix continued to ignore her as if her voice was only the annoying buzz of some passing insect.

"According to this book," he paused, looking at the title for the first time.

"*Manifestations of the Paranormal*," Melinda said.

"*Manifestations of the Paranormal*," Felix parroted, not paying the slightest attention to Melinda. "In a séance, mediums have been known to have ghostly images reflected in their eyes."

Melinda sighed. "I guess the idea of Indigo being a bit like Cerberus isn't so farfetched after all. Maybe she *is* connected to the Underworld—maybe Indigo can communicate with the dead."

CHAPTER ELEVEN

"What a strange name," Indigo said to the old man, as they walked up the path from the shore to a tiny white house where an old woman waited. The sun was high in the sky, which suggested that it was about midday, and the air was deliciously warm.

The old man laughed. "I suppose the name Utnapishtim seems strange to you now, but once upon a time you did not think it was so odd."

Indigo looked at him and smiled. He was very old but didn't walk with a stoop; he was tall and strong and proud. Indigo knew this man. She knew that he was kind and clever, wise and thoughtful. She knew that she had known him all her life, but for some reason she couldn't remember ever having heard his voice or seen his face before.

She was comfortable in this place—a place she'd visited a thousand times, but again, she couldn't remember ever having walked on this beach, with the shore grasses pushing through the sand, or the smell of the salty air and reflection of the shimmering crystal sea that stretched out for miles from the shore.

"Saba," the old man called to the old woman. "Look who has come for a visit."

The old woman squinted, then smiled. "Indigo, is that you? It has been such a long time, child." When they reached the porch, the old woman hugged Indigo, then held her face between her old wrinkled hands. She sighed. "Even though so many years have passed, I can't believe the time has come," she whispered as a single tear rolled down her smiling face.

Indigo nodded sadly. "It has," she agreed, although she couldn't remember what was about to happen.

"There's no need for you to be sad," laughed the old woman. "It is I who must be sad, for you are to continue your journey but I cannot follow—Anu has seen to that. But enough about that. *Níg-ge-na-da a-ba in-da-di nam-ti ì-ù-tu.*"

The call of a gull flying overhead startled Indigo just as everything turned very dark. She blinked only once, and when her eyes opened she was in her own room in her own bed. Aunt Phoebe stared at her from on top of the covers. The cat's face was only inches away, and for a second Indigo imagined that the corners of its whiskered mouth were turned up in a smile.

Melinda's eyes opened to total darkness, not to the brilliance of the sunshine that she had expected. The sound of the waves was gone. The cry of seagulls was replaced with the chirping of crickets. The air was dry and cool. She was alone. For a terrifying instant, she felt lost. Slowly her eyes focused and she was able to pick out the familiar objects in her room. She was in her bed, and from the blackness of the hour she knew she was meant to be asleep.

She rolled onto her back and stared up at the ceiling, not seeing the crack in the plaster or the spider who was diligently working on her web. What she saw instead was a white house surrounded by sand, where Indigo was talking to Dr. Zhang.

CHAPTER TWELVE

Felix sat up abruptly, blinking wildly as he searched through the darkness for a clue as to where he was. It didn't take him long to determine that he was safely where he was meant to be: in his bed, in his room—alone.

"It was only a dream," he exhaled, lying back against the pillow, feeling relieved but still very unsettled. The vivid image of one of Indigo's three heads reciting Chinese proverbs to her other two heads, who were enjoying lunch in the school's cafeteria, was so much clearer than the hazy quality his dreams normally had. He shook his head to dislodge the memory, then clicked on his lamp and picked up his glasses, which he had left on top of his late-night reading, *Tales of the Underworld*. A cartoon image of Cerberus, Hades's three-headed guard dog, stared up from the cover.

"This is insane," he groaned. "Indigo isn't some kind of freak. She *is* eccentric," he acknowledged, "but a lot of *really* clever people are." He thought about this for a few seconds, then continued in a resigned whisper, "I don't know what Melinda saw in her eyes, but I'm sure it was nothing. Mel just wants Indigo to be as weird as she is." With that, he yawned, put his glasses back on top of the book, and turned off the light.

Class was almost over, but Felix kept an eye on the doorway, expecting Indigo to walk in at any moment. It wasn't like her to be late, let alone to miss the first two lessons of the day. When the bell rang, Felix pushed through the mass of students, all trying to be the first through the narrow doorway, then hurried down the hall toward his next class. The passage was crowded with people, all jostling each other with armloads of books. Felix felt like a pinball, bouncing off body after body while he searched faces for Indigo's, when he heard his name almost whispered behind him.

He spun around immediately, expecting to see Indigo, but it was Harmony who seemed eager to get his attention. She stood in a statuesque pose about two meters away with a steely gaze that, to the other students, was nothing more than her manikin-like affect, but Felix could tell something was troubling her.

"Indigo is not at school today, but neither she nor her aunt contacted admissions to say why. Have you heard from her?" she asked in a shaky whisper.

"No, she's probably just late. I'll bet she's already in the physics lab."

Harmony sighed. "I'm afraid not. I just came from there."
She looked around at the crowded hallway. "Let's go into my
office where we can talk," she said softly, jerking her head.

Felix followed her into the large and simply furnished
office. At the far end, tall windows looked out on the gardens
at the front of the school. A massive red mahogany desk and
chair sat in front, facing the doorway, so that when Harmony
worked she sat with her back to the garden view. As usual,
her office was uncluttered; the only thing on her desk—in
fact, the only thing he had ever seen on top of her desk—was
a pen and pencil set given to her by her parents when she'd
graduated university.

Felix sat down in one of two gold upholstered chairs that
faced the desk. Harmony walked over to the windows, then
turned to face him. "I'm concerned about Indigo."

Felix shrugged. "She's probably not feeling well. When
she got to our house on Saturday, she was completely
drenched from walking through the rain—maybe she came
down with something."

Harmony continued, unconvinced. "I phoned the
number the admissions office had listed for her, but I was
told the number had been disconnected several years ago
and that it had been registered in the name of Pierre Verret."

Felix shrugged. "I don't know who Pierre Verret is; she
lives with her Aunt Phoebe and I don't think Indigo has a
phone. The office must have mixed something up."

Harmony shook her head. "There's more…Since I
know where she lives, I popped round during my break
this morning. I understand that her Aunt Phoebe is not in

good health, and if Indigo was sick I thought I'd see if they needed anything." She took a deep breath, her expression bewildered as she blurted out, "But it was gone."

Felix smiled nervously. "She was gone?"

Harmony frowned. "I didn't say she, I said *it*—and what I'm trying to say, without sounding absolutely mad, is that the building was gone."

"A building just doesn't disappear. You must have gone to the wrong address."

"I did not," Harmony snapped. "I went to the exact address I drove her to on Saturday; the same place where I escorted her up the stairs to her flat. I even waited until she unlocked the door to make sure she was safe."

Felix's skin felt damp and his voice began to quiver. "Are you saying that they demolished it?"

Harmony met Felix's eyes, slowly shaking her head. "It wasn't demolished. It simply wasn't there. I went into the *patisserie* a short distance away and talked to the owner. The woman knew the building very well, describing some of the same architectural details that I had admired when I was there on Saturday. It seems this particular building is well known...it's quite a landmark in architectural circles." She turned away from Felix and faced the windows. "She thought that's why I was looking for it, because I had read something about it. When I said I had been to the building just a couple of days earlier and that a girl who attended the school lived there, she started to laugh." She faced Felix again. "The owner of the *patisserie* told me the building had been completely destroyed by a fire more than ten years ago, and that the site where it stood has been a vacant lot ever since."

The door burst open and Professor Mulligan stormed in. "Harmony," he barked, a little out of breath, "I think I must have left my notes in here, the ones I need for the meeting with the board of directors." He stopped when he noticed Felix, "Oh, I am sorry. I didn't know you were busy."

Harmony motioned for him to shut the door and join them. "Felix and I were just talking about Indigo, and I'm a bit…"

Mulligan shook his head and held up a hand. "I'm sorry, I really don't have the time to discuss any student's failing grades or teenage problems."

Harmony raised a single eyebrow. "I can assure you neither of those apply to Indigo Jasper, and if you'll just listen a minute—"

Professor Mulligan shook his head violently. "I am sorry, but it's simply not a good time to discuss anything about one of the students—the board is convening in just under an hour, and I have lost my notes. If you don't have them, then I must have left them someplace else." He shook his head and sighed. "You don't know how difficult these meetings are," he moaned, looking at Felix. "I do wish you would attend as Stumpworthy one day; it would really take the pressure off me, having to invent excuses about why he can't attend. I'm afraid I'm running low on plausible explanations, and I think the board members are getting a little fed up with him—he's still the owner of this school, you know." Without waiting for a reply, he pivoted and stormed back toward the door, stopping just short of exiting. He turned back to face them and sighed again. "I apologize if I am being rude, I just get a little flustered with this type of thing. After the meeting, I promise, I would be happy to talk about this...ah...Imogen with you."

"Indigo Jasper," Felix said slowly, as if talking to a small child. "Smartest girl in school...winner of the Science School of Excellence Gold Award last year."

The professor looked from Felix to Harmony, then back at Felix. "To my recollection, I have never met *anyone* named Indigo." The grave look on his face sent shivers up Felix's back. "And you know very well, Felix, that you won the Science School's Gold Award last year."

CHAPTER THIRTEEN

Felix felt numb as he looked out across the vacant lot. The only evidence that a building had once stood here was the pile of rubble at the far corner of the property. Other than that, the ground was a sea of tall grasses and weeds, interrupted only by colorful splotches of rubbish. All around him, Parisian life trudged along normally: people hurried homeward carrying baguettes under their arms and sirens blared in the distance. But Felix felt like he was acting in a sci-fi thriller where he was one of the only two people left alive.

Harmony sighed and asked in a pitiful moan, "How is it possible that an entire building simply vanishes?"

"It isn't," Felix decided, pushing his glasses back up to the bridge of his nose.

Harmony nodded slowly, returning her gaze to the vacant plot. "I must have made a mistake—I can't imagine how, but it's obvious that nothing has stood on this spot for a very long time." She shook her head slowly. "What about Indigo—did she exist, or did I imagine her as well?"

Felix shrugged. "If she did exist, then you and I are the only ones who knew her. It's not just Mulligan—none of her records were in the office, and she wasn't even in the class photo." He spat the words out, then rubbed his forehead. "The weird part is that I remember standing next to her for that picture. But you saw for yourself: Indigo Jasper was not in that photograph!" He blinked several times to push back the tears, then looked up at Harmony, who seemed mesmerized by a piece of paper fluttering across the lot.

"You didn't see the building, so of course you can't imagine that it was here only days ago. But we shouldn't start questioning the reality of Indigo. We both knew her; she is…" Harmony paused. "Well, at least she *was* real."

"Real in our minds, at least." Felix sighed. "Either we're sharing the same hallucination, or some unbelievably powerful force wiped out everyone else's memory of her."

"Like that movie about the people who worked with aliens—didn't they destroy people's memories?" Harmony chuckled softly.

"I haven't seen any men in black suits and sunglasses running around," Felix muttered. "Maybe it's an Athenite thing—something connected to our ability to read thoughts. Is it possible we shared a dream that's now registered in our brains as a memory?"

Harmony smiled sadly. "Maybe," she said absently. "People who suffer from delusions often can't tell reality from their own imaginings, and sometimes those delusional thoughts are recorded in their brains as memories. But I've never heard of two people sharing the same hallucination."

The library was quiet except for the gasp Melinda made when she looked down at her clawed feet. Even though she stood seven feet above them, they looked huge. Next she admired herself in the mirror above the fireplace. Amber-colored eyes and tawny fur highlighted her lion's face; frighteningly sharp white teeth were the picture of dragon-like perfection. The rest of her body that was still that of a twelve-year old girl— albeit a very tall, furry one.

She spun around girlishly, which did not suit the terrifying image of the creature she had morphed into, then scampered out of the room and down the hallway. Reaching the foyer, she pranced around in delight for a heady moment before assuming a cat-like perch directly across from the door. Felix was due home at any minute.

Melinda yawned as the minutes passed. By the time the front door did open, half an hour later, her chin had settled on her chest and long streams of thick drool cascaded from the corners of her mouth. At the door's creak, her eyes rolled open and she stiffly stood up, stretching to her full seven-foot height.

"ARGH!" howled James Mulligan at the spectacle of the beast in front of him. He staggered sideways against the wall and then slid down into an unrespectable heap on the floor.

"It's only me," groaned Melinda, but to Mulligan's ears this sounded like vicious, man-eating growls.

"James, what on earth is the matter?" Harmony cried, stepping in with Felix behind her. She glanced over at Melinda, who struck her as almost comical, and gave a heavy sigh. "Oh, for Heaven's sake, James, it's only Melinda."

James Mulligan slowly shook his head. "Of course it's Melinda," he barked. "But I would be most grateful if, just once, I could walk in through the front door without suffering a stroke!"

Harmony groaned under the professor's considerable weight as she helped him to his feet. Then, with a look that shouted how displeased she was to be a human crutch, she escorted him up the stairs.

Felix smiled for the first time all day. "The old goat deserved it," he whispered, still resentful of the professor's inability to remember Indigo. "Good one, Mel. I don't know what you're supposed to be, but whatever it is, good job."

Melinda flashed a frighteningly toothy grin that faded the second Felix's thoughts filtered into her head. "Why did Walrus face say he doesn't know Indigo?" she growled.

Felix shook his head. "You know I can't understand you when you're a different species."

Within seconds, Melinda stood naked in front of him. "I read your mind," she said matter-of-factly. "What's going on with Indigo?"

"PUT SOME CLOTHES ON," he raged as he turned and marched toward the library, then abruptly skidded to a stop and spun back around. "You said Indigo! Do you know who she is?"

Melinda rolled her eyes as she struggled into a huge red raincoat from the hall closet. "What are you talking about? Of course I know her, she was here all day Saturday." Felix stared at his sister for several seconds, the day's events whirling through his head. An instant later, Melinda knew the whole story. "That *is* weird," she said with a click of her tongue.

Felix nodded. "No one except you, me, and Harmony can remember anything about Indigo Jasper," he said.

"Maybe she *is* on that island," Melinda mused aloud, and though Felix had no clue what she meant by that, he felt his heart jump nonetheless.

CHAPTER FOURTEEN

"Paradise Shore," Melinda rattled as she hurried into her clothes that she had left on the floor in the library.

"What are you talking about?" Felix asked with an exasperated sigh.

"Indigo. She was talking to Dr. Zhang." She paused, shaking her head slightly. "But he didn't really look like Dr. Zhang, and Indigo called him Utnappy-something. Anyway, in my dream Dr. Zhang had a wife called Saba." At the word *dream*, Felix's head drooped, and his spirit with it, wondering why he ever bothered to listen to Melinda. But his sister apparently wasn't done, still rattling on about her wild imagination. "I could tell they'd known Indigo for a really long time; they said she had to continue on her journey." She pulled on her jeans and socks in silence, then continued with a puzzled expression: "You know what was really strange about this dream? I wasn't in it. I mean I was, because I could see what was going on, but it's like I was invisible. No one noticed me."

Felix wished he could make her disappear now. "You're talking about one of your ridiculous dreams," he groaned, turning away and walking over to the desk.

Melinda shot him an irritated glare. "When I woke up, I remembered everything. It was like some of the other dreams I've had—the ones that were real. I told Mum about it this morning, and she said it sounded like the story of *Gilgamesh*. It's a Sumerian story," she announced proudly, "written more than two thousand years ago and recorded on twelve stone tablets. I read Mom's translated copy today, and those people in my dream were in the story! So was Huwawa."

"Whatever," Felix mumbled, trying to shut out the sound of her voice.

"Huwawa was the Guardian of the Forest—that's who I was when you came home," she said ominously, waiting for a reaction. But it was obvious that Felix had successfully blocked her out. Anger rose up quickly as she stomped over to the desk, slapped her hands down on the papers he was shuffling through, and leaned in until the surprised breath from his nostrils swept across her cheeks. "Look, Felix, I don't know why I dreamt about Indigo and those people, but it can't be a coincidence that I had that dream and now Indigo is gone and you don't know where she is. You're even wondering if she was real at all, which is really stupid because you know she is."

Felix finally looked up with a hopeful expression. "How can you be so sure?"

Melinda's eyes twinkled. "I told you she wasn't human. So whatever has happened to her might be perfectly normal for whatever she is. Now you just have to figure that out, and then you might be able to find her."

It was well after midnight, but unlike the rest of the household, Felix couldn't sleep. Normally he wouldn't have heard the car engine as it drove up the driveway or the click of the front door slipping shut. Without switching on the light, he fumbled for his robe and hurried out into the hall and down the stairs.

The foyer was dark, illuminated only by a subtle light coming from the library. Felix almost ran toward the light, feeling inexplicably that answers to questions about Indigo might be only seconds away.

Joe Whiltshire was kneeling in front of the fireplace, trying to revive the dwindling fire with a poker. He had been away for weeks.

Joe turned his head and smiled, not at all startled by Felix's arrival. "I'm getting pretty good at this," he chuckled. "I had a strong sense you would be joining me. I've been practicing my telepathy." He turned back to the fire, which was sparking with new life, then stood and faced Felix.

Felix never ceased to be in awe of the man in front of him. No matter what the circumstance or his attire, Joe Whiltshire's rugged good looks always made him look a little like a movie hero.

"My flight was late…we only landed a couple of hours ago, and then there was such a hassle with passport control and customs. Travel has become so difficult I've been thinking about transforming and flying on my own. If I can figure out a way to do it without confusing the museum, that is—they make all my travel arrangements." Joe paused when he noticed the concerned look on Felix's face. It was obvious Felix was not there to discuss his travel options. "What has you awake at this hour?" Joe asked as he took a seat on the center sofa facing the fireplace.

Felix wanted to launch into the myriad questions he felt sure Joe could answer, but he managed to hold himself back. "How was your dig?"

Joe stared intently at Felix for a few seconds. "I'm quite certain that's not why you're here, but thanks for asking anyway. We've made a lot of progress and found some incredible artifacts. I'm here because I was needed back at the museum, but I'll be heading back to South America as soon as I can."

He waited for Felix to ask something else, maybe about the prized Chilean stone monkey or the unusual Incan mask that had the archeological society reeling with excitement. Felix didn't; something else was on his mind, and Joe smiled as he deciphered the boy's thoughts.

"I see," Joe began, "you're interested in…" He paused, then squinted as he searched Felix's mind. "A color… violet…that you might find on an island…no, no…it's not a color that you want to find, it's a rock! You want to know about an igneous rock found at the seashore." He sat back and smiled proudly, convinced, even though it made no sense, that he had successfully read Felix's mind.

Felix curled his lips, shaking his head as he looked at Joe, who seemed a little less like a hero at the moment. "No, I was…"

"Sumerian," Joe interrupted. "Islands that have Chinese teachers…Felix, you're not making any sense!"

Felix shook his head. "You mean *you're* not making any sense," he snorted. "Maybe you should let me tell you what's on my mind." Joe looked slightly rebuffed, but he didn't get a chance to reply before Felix launched into his explanation about Indigo's disappearance.

Joe nodded. "Well, that makes more sense…in a way. Not that I can help you with disappearing buildings or girls that exist only in a few people's minds. I've never come across anything like this before."

Felix looked down at his clasped hands. "There's one other thing that might be a clue, but…it makes even less sense." He paused and took a deep breath—then, cheeks reddening, he told Joe about the ghosts Melinda claimed to have seen in Indigo's eyes and about Melinda's dream in as much detail he could recall.

Joe leaned forward, resting his elbows on his knees and cradling his chin with his thumbs. His frown deepened with every word of Felix's explanation. When Felix had finished, Joe didn't move, not saying a word for a long moment before he shook his head in disbelief and rocked back against the sofa. "That sounds a lot like the Sumerian version of *Gilgamesh*. We believe it had been told by other civilizations for hundreds of years—nomadic people and sailors probably recited it for entertainment, changing it to suit their environment, not unlike the way we remake movies for new audiences today. For instance, stories about a great flood have been told by countless civilizations, in theory to explain why seashells were found on mountaintops…"

Felix shook his head. "I don't care about the story," he moaned. "Could any of that be a clue about Indigo? Who she is—and more importantly, where she is?" He sighed, looking over at the clock and noticing it was almost two in the morning. Joe would be off to work at the museum in just a few hours. This might be his only chance to have Joe's undivided attention for a long time. "Wait here," he commanded, then jumped to his feet and ran from the room, mumbling to himself, "This has got to be one of the stupidest ideas I've ever had."

CHAPTER FIFTEEN

Felix guided a drowsy Melinda to the library and left her to stumble into the room so he could take up his seat on the sofa. The glow from the fire reflecting off her dark, curly hair made it look like a mop of writhing brown serpents. Her eyes were puffy and only half open; she looked bewildered, as if she was walking in her sleep. She shuffled groggily after Felix until she noticed the blurred image of Joe directly in front of her. She didn't open her mouth or make a sound, but her voice sang a cheerful hello in his mind.

"You don't have to say anything," she slurred through a wide yawn when she read his thoughts, which at that moment were consumed with questions of whether he should think or speak his response. "I always know what you're thinking."

Joe nodded, remembering the special connection he shared with her. "It still takes some getting used to," he said aloud. "I'm sure that Felix and your dad forget their connection at times. I spend so much time practicing telepathy that I forget about the mind connection some Athenites share."

"Which is exactly why she's here," Felix interrupted. "Melinda can tell you everything she saw in Indigo's eyes and in her dream simply by sending you her thoughts."

Joe's face lit up with a *that's-a-brilliant-suggestion* expression, and seconds later there was a picture of Indigo in his mind, registering like a memory of someone he had known. He recognized her face and knew the sound of her voice and the way she moved. He looked into her velvety brown eyes and saw the ghosts Felix had tried to describe. Then he was plunged into a dream, a dream that seemed to have belonged to him. He saw the sea and the white clapboard house on the shore, where Indigo was talking with Utnapishtim.

Melinda stretched across the sofa and closed her eyes. "He didn't look like Dr. Zhang in my dream, but I know it was him. You can meet him tomorrow; I have my lesson at 3:00," she whispered through another yawn.

Joe nodded. "That's a good idea. I don't know how he fits into this, or even if he does, but it couldn't hurt to say hello." Melinda nodded absently before rolling over in an attempt to go back to sleep.

"How about you, Felix? Do you have any extraordinary information about Indigo that might help us solve this mystery?"

Felix didn't answer immediately as he searched his memories for something that might be useful. After a few seconds, he looked up excitedly. "A few weeks ago Indigo had to leave the classroom because she looked like she was about to faint; I helped her out into the hallway. As soon as we left the room, I noticed a horrible rash on her neck.

I'm not kidding—her neck was covered in blisters and dead skin," he said, still amazed at the image in his mind. "She didn't even know it was there until I asked her what it was. Then just like that—" He snapped his fingers. "—it was gone."

Joe leaned forward with a concerned expression. "That is strange. I just wish I had any idea what it meant."

Melinda strained to look past the wire-rimmed spectacles, trying to see into the narrow, dark eyes of Dr. Zhang. It was difficult to get a clear view from where she was sitting, especially since he hadn't glanced up during the entire lesson.

"You seem distracted today," he said, looking down at a book that he held in his lap. "Is something troubling you?"

Melinda sat straight up, first shaking her head and then nodding in resignation. "Actually, I can't figure out something. The other night I dreamt about something kind of weird, and you were in my dream."

The corners of Dr. Zhang's mouth twitched ever so slightly upward. "You told me some time ago that you enjoy fables," he said, as if she hadn't spoken. He raised his head, still not meeting her eyes. "That is why I have brought you this book. In English, it is called *The Dreams of Min Min*. It is a wonderful story about a girl who travels to the land of the dead through her dreams. In China, it is believed that the *hun*— that is what we call the spiritual soul—leaves the body during a dream to communicate with the dead." He offered

Melinda the book, meeting her eyes for the first time. "Min Min learns much about the past, her ancestry, and finally her future as she sorts out the mysteries of the underworld and discovers that death need not be the end, but can in fact be the beginning."

Melinda eyed him curiously, then gingerly took hold of the book. The only thing on its cover was a Chinese character.

"That is the character for *The Chinese Dream*," Dr. Zhang explained.

Melinda looked up from the book, again meeting his eyes, and smiled. "It's funny that I can never tell what you're thinking," she said, then in almost a whisper asked, "Did you know I had a dream about you before I told you? Is that why you brought me this book?"

A few seconds passed before he answered, "Perhaps on some level I did. It is strange how two minds can be linked with similar thoughts at the same time. But perhaps it wasn't that *I* knew about your dream; perhaps your dream foretold the future. Many cultures believe that…"

"The ancient Egyptians, for one, believed dreams held the key to the future," announced Joe as he strode into the room. "Hi, I'm Joe Whiltshire," he said, walking toward Dr. Zhang with his hand extended in greeting.

"Ah, Dr. Whiltshire," Dr. Zhang said pleasantly as he took Joe's hand. "Melinda has told me about your work, especially as it pertains to China. She has been fortunate to have experienced life in such a way: living around the world and learning real history from such a famous archeologist as yourself."

Joe absently looked at his watch, then back at Dr. Zhang. "I hope I'm not interrupting your lesson."

Dr. Zhang shook his head. "We were just finishing. In fact, we deviated slightly from our discussion to talk about dreams."

"So I heard." Joe winked at Melinda. "It is an interesting topic. In the seventh century BC, King Ashurbanipal gave careful attention to dreams and kept records of them; if memory serves me, the earliest records date back more than three thousand years."

A rare smile lightened Dr. Zhang's expression. "Yes, I believe I recall reading something about that. Wasn't there an ancient poem where a Sumerian king described a recurring dream to his mother?"

Joe took a deep breath and nodded. "You must be referring to the story of Gilgamesh. In the story, Gilgamesh's dreams were taken as prophecy." He looked over at Melinda, hoping she'd get his telepathic message to read the doctor's mind. "Isn't it odd that you should mention that story?" Joe smiled. "Melinda and I have been talking about it lately."

"Perhaps it is odd, or perhaps it is more evidence of mind connections that exist between people of like-mindedness." Dr. Zhang bowed his head solemnly. "*Jiu niu yi mao*," he said softly.

"'Loss of one hair from nine oxen.'" Melinda bowed back. "I have a feeling that it is."

Even before the front door clicked shut, Melinda peered out through the long, tall window on the side of the door to watch Dr. Zhang shuffle down the steps and walk purposefully down the driveway. He always walked. He never arrived in a car and never left in a car, always saying he had no need for such convenience since his legs could carry him very well. It was fortunate, Melinda thought, that so far it had not rained on lesson days.

She waited a few more minutes to make sure Dr. Zhang would not be able to read her mind, even though she wasn't sure he could. She turned around slowly, her eyes darting this way and that to make sure she was absolutely alone; she didn't want anyone to know her thoughts just yet, at least not until she understood them herself.

She shook the image of the nine oxen out of her head and began concentrating on the images she'd seen in the doctor's eyes as she ambled down the passage.

"Were you able to read his mind?" Joe asked eagerly when she walked back into the library.

Melinda shrugged. "I guess so, but the only things I could read were exactly the things that he said."

"You must know something else. I can sense it," Joe said proudly. "And what's with the hairy ox comment?"

"*Loss of one hair from nine oxen* is an old Chinese proverb about how something small or insignificant can actually be something very important. He's always using proverbs to explain things. He says they describe the past as well as the future." She looked at the blank expression on Joe's face and sighed.

"Whatever," Joe said, shaking his head. "What I find interesting is that he brought up the story of Gilgamesh. Had you described your dream to him in any detail?" Melinda shook her head. "It just seems a strange coincidence. You were talking about dreams, and the next thing you know he starts spouting off about Gilgamesh—the dream was only a small part of that story, so why would it come to mind? Are you sure there was nothing else on his mind?"

Melinda sighed again and shook her head. "Nothing on his mind, but there was something really weird in his eyes. At first I couldn't see very much because he never looked up, and what little I could see looked like the same kind of reflection I always see when I look into a human's eyes. But when he gave me this book," she said, holding it out for Joe to see, "he looked me straight in the eye." She paused.

"And?" Joe prodded. "What did you see?"

"I saw my reflections," she said in a puzzled tone.

"You saw yourself?"

Again she shook her head. "Not *my* reflection—the reflections of my *thoughts*."

CHAPTER SIXTEEN

The slow dusk brought a coppery glow to the library. Joe had left for the museum, saying he would return the next day. Felix's brain felt tight in his skull, and listening to Melinda wasn't helping.

"I agree that Gilgamesh thing is quite a coincidence, but I'm sure that's all it is: a coincidence. And I'll admit that what you saw in Dr. Zhang's eyes was unusual, but how does he fit into this?"

"I don't know if he does. Joe said to include everything in our investigation, so I am. You heard him—he wants us to piece together all the clues that we have so far. Tomorrow we can talk to Harmony again; then, when we have more of a direction to follow, we can involve Mum. So far we have links to Chinese and Sumerian mythology, dreams as they relate to reality, and disappearing people...and buildings."

Felix took off his glasses and rubbed his eyes. "It's like we're trying to force together a puzzle but we don't have all the pieces, and the ones we do have don't fit together."

After three more hours hunched over his computer in the library, Felix's eyes were burning and his back ached.

"This is nuts," he groaned. "I did a search on *legends about people who disappear* and I got five websites about the sightings of Elvis Presley; three sites about the disappearance of Atlantis; one site about the author Franz Kafka, who apparently wanted to disappear; and, last and probably least, several stories about people who were convinced they had disappeared only to reappear again within seconds, telling anyone who would listen about how the devil himself had summoned them to the underworld."

He met Melinda's eyes from over the top of *The Poetic Edda and Other Norse Myths*, which rested on her chest as she reclined comfortably on a sofa.

"I've been running searches on every clue we have," he continued, "and haven't come up with anything useful. I think the problem is that the one piece of information I need to make this an intelligent search is the one piece I'm searching *for*." He leaned forward and stared at the computer screen for another couple of minutes—then, as if inspiration had finally struck, began typing up a storm.

Melinda immediately lost herself in the pages of the ancient Norse stories. She was so engrossed in a story about a mighty horned beast that she didn't notice when thick, sturdy horns began to grow out of the top of her head. And she was equally unaware that tusks protruded out of the corners of her mouth when she read about Ottar, who had taken the form of a boar. She had become so lost in the imagery of the fables that she had completely forgotten why she was reading the book until she got to the story of Baldur's Dream.

She snapped the book closed and sat up, looking guiltily over at Felix. He looked tired and frail; his skin had taken on a sickly, greenish pallor in the reflection off the computer screen. He was working so hard and she had just been enjoying reading.

"Did you find anything?" Felix asked as he looked over at his sister. When he saw her horns and tusks, he rolled his eyes. "You are an idiot," he said, exasperated.

Melinda's face went red, thinking for a second that he had caught her out. "There is a reference to dreams, but nothing else," she said, trying to sound exhausted. She stood stiffly, gathering up the other three books she had already skimmed. Her arms heavy with the weight of the thick volumes, she waddled over to the stairs that led up to the third floor.

Felix watched as his horned sister plodded up the stairs and then turned his attention back to his work. He usually told Melinda about unwanted animal appendages, but he was just out of sorts enough to let her discover them for herself.

She replaced the first two books in their proper places on the shelves, but when she attempted to slide the last book into its slot she found she couldn't push it all the way in. She tried jamming it, wiggling it, and finally thrusting with every ounce of strength she could muster, but it would not go. Finally leaning forward and peering into the gap, she saw a small book blocking the way.

"Stupid book," she seethed, sliding her hand into the narrow space and removing the little book. She slipped the other book smoothly into place before glancing at the volume in her hand. Its brown leather cover was old and worn. There wasn't a title, nor any identifying marks on the spine. She opened the front cover, gasped, and closed it immediately, only to reopen it again eagerly a second later.

Below her, Felix shook his head, removed his glasses, and massaged his eyes. "That's enough for tonight...I'm not getting anywhere," he called, glancing up at Melinda's horned head bobbing along the aisle on the third floor.

"Felix, you've got to read this!" she giggled excitedly. "It's Stumpworthy's diary, and it's all about his girlfriends! I can't believe he was ever a *lover boy*," she drawled as she bounded down the stairs.

A sickening knot gripped Felix's stomach. He didn't want to think about the professor at all, let alone in a romantic scene. "I can't believe you read his diary. That's rude."

"I didn't read that much," she said huffily, tossing him the diary. Then she scooped up the enthralling book of Norse stories and scampered out of the library.

Felix looked down at the little journal with the intention of throwing it into the bin—but instead, without quite knowing why, he clutched it tightly, clicked off the light, and went upstairs to his room.

CHAPTER SEVENTEEN

Felix's head hadn't creased the pillow before he was sitting upright again, reading lamp on and the diary in his hands. This was the third time the temptation to look inside had won out over sleep. Gingerly, he opened the cover and began reading the recollections of Professor Horace Stumpworthy.

After all this time, how could I be so certain it was her? I haven't seen Millicent for at least fifteen years, since she moved away. It was so painful to have her virtually disappear from my life. Funny how a fourteen-year-old boy reacts to things! I had such a wild crush on her, and she never even knew it. We were friends and study partners and that was that.

Felix shuddered, shaking his head violently to dislodge the feeling that somehow he and the professor had shared the exact same experience. He skipped a few pages.

But that woman, the one who interviewed at the lab, the one called Helen. She reminded me so much of Millicent. She looked nothing like her, but people change when they grow up. Me, for instance—I was such a scrawny lad, and now I'm over six feet tall and, I'm told, cut a rather dashing figure.

The next entry was dated a week later:

I don't know what I was thinking—how could Helen possibly be Millicent? I can always tell by the eyes, and Millicent's were different. I can hardly remember now what I used to imagine seeing when I looked into those big green eyes, but the fact is they were green and Helen's are most definitely brown. Now it's time to be honest: Millicent was an extraordinary girl who has held a place in my heart for many years, but it's long past time to let her go.

Felix looked up from the page; a cold sweat soaked his pajamas. There was something too familiar about the professor's recollections. Was he simply finding similarities with his own situation, or could it be that he was living in parallel to Stumpworthy's past? He returned to the diary and continued to read about Helen, each page making him feel an overwhelming sense of familiarity. Then he read a passage that caught his breath in his throat.

I saw the strangest images in Helen's eyes. Cloudy images, like opaque reflections of people, but there were no other people in the room. There was something familiar about those ghostly shadows, and for some reason they made me feel happy. Then I remembered: those were the same images I once saw in Millicent's eyes.

Felix gaped at the open page. "Cloudy images just like Indigo? It can't be."

Joe Whiltshire yawned as he made his way up the dark steps to the front door of the mansion. It was just past three a.m., and he had been working continuously for the last thirty-six hours. He felt exhausted but content: his project at the museum was finished, and he was eager to get back to the dig. But at the moment, all he wanted to think about now was a quiet hot bath and long sleep. In fact, he thought he might sleep through the next couple of days entirely.

Before he had had a chance to reach for his key the front door burst open and Felix, wide eyed and agitated, sprang out at him.

"Joe, do you think Stumpworthy might have known Indigo…ah…before?"

Joe stepped inside and stared at Felix for a full minute before answering. "He's the one who invited her to join his school. We all know the story—it was at the same time you came to the school, only a few months before Horace left this world," Joe said, finding it difficult to suppress a smile at the memory of Stumpworthy's demise.

Felix shook his head. Joe slipped by him into the house, and Felix shut the door and followed Joe up the stairs, undeterred. "He described her in his diary."

Joe stopped and turned slowly to face him. "Why would Horace be writing about a student in his diary?"

"Not Indigo exactly." Felix held the journal out. "You've got to read it."

Joe eyed the little leather-bound book before taking it reluctantly. "Let me take a look, and then we'll talk. But right now, I'm going up to bed, and you should do the same."

Not more than fifteen minutes later, it was Joe's turn to barrel into Felix's room. "Where did you find this?" he demanded, no longer showing any sign of exhaustion.

Felix sat up and tucked his arms around his knees. "Melinda found it, actually. In the library. Why?"

Joe crossed the room to look out at the inky sky, only the city lights breaking the vast swath of darkness. "I had almost forgotten about Helen." He scrubbed a hand through his hair and pivoted to face Felix again. "Horace was in love with her."

"I know."

"It was her disappearance that was strange."

The hairs on the back of Felix's neck bristled. "She disappeared?"

Joe nodded. "Without a trace. It was like she simply vanished. No one even remembered her except a few of us."

"Just like Indigo," Felix said in a quaking voice.

Joe crossed his arms over his chest. "Horace used to rave about it. He was convinced Helen was the same person as the girl he had the crush on when he was a kid."

"Millicent."

Again Joe nodded. "He said he'd seen the same images in both of their eyes."

"The same images Melinda said she saw in Indigo's."

"Sounds that way."

"So what does that mean for Indigo? Do you think she's the same person?" Felix asked hesitantly, hoping the answer would be no.

"It's quite probable, but we can't be sure. It would help if we could find any research Horace might have done. He was fascinated with both Millicent and Helen, and would have tried to learn more, which might have led to finding them—or *her*. I need to reconnect with Melinda about the images she saw in Indigo's eyes. Then we might be able to piece this together, and perhaps discover where Indigo has gone."

"I'll get Melinda," Felix said, already making for the door.

"Don't wake her," Joe urged. "She'll be up in a few hours; we can ask her then. Right now, I'm trying to remember something Horace told me. He was close to discovering the woman's origin when something drastic happened, but I can't remember what it was," he said. "I have the sense there's an ancient tale about people like her, but I can't even remember that—something about people who travel through time and space, beings that look like humans and have a biological makeup that matches a human being." He banged his fist against the windowsill. "Why can't I remember! All I can recall is that something horrible had happened." He helplessly shook his head.

Felix looked at the floor then up into Joe's eyes. "Maybe there's a way Melinda can help you remember. Since she can transfer her thoughts to you, maybe she can also access your memory."

Joe nodded but then bit his lip. "The problem is that I don't know how to send her a thought I can't even recall."

Felix stared out across his bedroom. In the corner of the room, he saw several black rice-shaped kernels, the unmistakable droppings of a mouse. He cringed slightly, wondering if he should ask Melinda to change into a cat and deal with the problem, but that thought just made him more squeamish. "What is it about mice?" he mumbled. "They're

so small, but everyone is afraid of them—even elephants."
He smirked.

"I think you need some rest," Joe urged as he shuffled
backward toward the door.

"That's it!" Felix said excitedly. "Remember that silly
superstition about mice scaring away elephants?" Joe looked
at him oddly and Felix held up his hands. "I know this
sounds crazy—maybe I am tired and my mind is wandering,
but when I started thinking about how frightened everyone
is about mice in the house, I began to wonder if it's true that
elephants are frightened of them. They probably aren't, but
it got me thinking about elephants, anyway. Do you think it's
true that *an elephant never forgets*?"

Joe's shoulders drooped. "You had better go to bed.
I'm afraid you might be suffering from sleep deprivation—
perhaps just a wee bit delusional."

"No, I'm not," Felix said defiantly. "Don't you get it?
If you changed into an elephant, you might remember
everything—everything Stumpworthy told you."

CHAPTER EIGHTEEN

Joe left Felix's room without another word, clicking the door shut behind him.

"He thinks I'm insane," Felix moaned. He shuffled over to his bed, not sleepy enough anymore to crawl back under the covers but not sure what else to do, when he heard someone out in the hallway. He rushed to the door, startling Melinda as he pulled it open. "What are you doing up so late?" he demanded.

"I could ask you the same thing," she whispered huffily. "You nearly gave me a heart attack."

Felix rolled his eyes. "What are you doing skulking around out here?" he asked again.

"I'm just going down to the kitchen to get a glass of milk, as if it's any of your business." She squared her shoulders, spun back around, and left.

Felix clicked his door shut again. The bed was cold and he was not tired but he crawled under the covers anyway. He picked up a copy of his biology book from the bedside table, hoping that would put him in a drowsy mood. He read three chapters, engrossed in every word, before he finally gave up. "It's no use," he sighed. "I need something boring to read if I'm going to fall asleep." He looked around for a novel, perhaps a crime thriller or something else that would give his brain little fodder, when a tremendous crash sounded from downstairs.

Every door in the hallway swung open at once. His mother ran into the passage, her hair wild around her head. Harmony joined her almost immediately and Professor Mulligan reluctantly poked his head out of his room to ask in a disgruntled tone, "What is all this commotion about…and at this hour?" Each of them struggled to wrap themselves in their robes; then, as a huddled mass, they moved cautiously toward the staircase. Felix hesitated only a few seconds before running to join the others. When they reached the top of the stairs, they gave a collective gasp and Felix couldn't stop himself from shouting, "MELINDA?"

In the center of the foyer, an elephant-like creature with Melinda's blue eyes and freckled cheeks stood next to the gigantic statue of the god Bes, which lay on its side. Its hideous head was severed and had rolled about two meters away.

Melinda looked up when she heard their scream and shook her head, her large elephant ears flapping with the movement.

No one said a word, all struggling with the same confusion as to why Melinda had decided to transform into an elephant in the middle of the foyer, in the middle of the night. No one found the words to ask before Joe stepped out of the shadows, adjusting his nightshirt and looking sheepishly up at their gaping faces.

"I'm afraid this was my fault," he said. He glanced down at his watch and motioned for everyone to join him downstairs. "It's almost six o'clock, and I doubt if any of us will be able to get much sleep after all this. Let's go into the library so I can explain."

"I figured the foyer was a safe place to transform," Joe admitted, shamefaced. "There's enough space for at least four elephants; what was the harm in only one? Melinda saw me as she came down the stairs and decided to transform as well. I had not seen her, but I heard something behind me and turned a little too quickly, and that's when I bumped into Bes."

"Why did the two of you decided to become elephants in the middle of the night?" Elaine asked impatiently.

"And in the middle of the house!" Mulligan added, incredulous.

"To remember," Melinda answered, as if that should explain everything.

Felix's face burnt with embarrassment. "It's my fault. I told Joe he might have better luck remembering things if he was an elephant."

Harmony looked more angry than confused. "This is nuts. A priceless statue has been destroyed, and you all did this to remember *things*? You know 'the elephant never forgets' is just a saying, don't you?"

"I remembered loads of stuff," Melinda defended. "Like when I was four and a neighborhood dog stole my shoe... Mum didn't believe me, but it happened! And when I was two, I know Felix had a bigger ice cream cone than I did! Not to mention all the long division that poured into my head..."

Joe smiled at Melinda, who had almost returned to her full human form except her nose still looked a bit like a trunk. "It wasn't just to remember *things*—it was to remember specific things Horace told me years ago about a woman he had been in love with."

Harmony's head dropped back against the couch. "Who cares about the man's wilted love life!"

"Knowing what happened to her might give us a clue about what happened to Indigo," Felix hurried to explain. "Melinda found Stumpworthy's diary, and there are things written in it about a woman named Helen and a girl named Millicent that are identical to things about Indigo, including her disappearance. Joe was hoping to remember something that might give us more information...information that might lead us to Indigo."

"It worked," Joe said proudly. "I remembered everything, so if you'll bear with me, I'll explain.

"There was a third woman, by the name of Courtney, who came into Horace's life after Helen disappeared. He was convinced that she, Millicent, and Helen were the same person. In those days, we were still great friends, so he confided in me. He told me they shared all the same characteristics of personality and intelligence, but that each one looked completely different. He also said that each of them had incredible knowledge about any subject that might come up."

"Just like Indigo," Felix added excitedly.

"Exactly," Joe nodded, "and this knowledge seemed to go beyond the bounds of normal study. Helen surprised Horace one time with her knowledge of Swahili and Courtney her complete understanding of Sanskrit, the ancient language used by Buddhist monks in the eighth century. I had met a lot of scholars in my time, but I had never heard of anyone with such breadth of knowledge. It was as if they had spent their short lives traveling and studying around the world, but each had insisted they had never been out of Paris."

"And you saw the ghosts!" Melinda called out excitedly.

Joe shook his head. "I only remembered what Horace described to me."

Elaine looked over at Felix. "You mentioned this—is it the same thing that Melinda saw in Indigo's eyes?"

Felix shrugged. "I think so, but it's impossible to be 100% sure. When Melinda and I researched the subject, I'm afraid we didn't find any stories about ghosts reflected in anyone's eyes, or anything even close." He looked hopefully at his mother. "Now that you know more about all of this, any old stories come to mind about women bouncing in and out of time, gathering knowledge, who might have something strange about their eyes?"

Elaine's lips curled. "From what I've read about time travel—which isn't much, I'll admit—those stories are usually the product of imagination, like *The Time Machine* or *A Wrinkle in Time*. Both are brilliant books, but definitely fiction." She paused, then, a little less certainly, added, "At least, I always thought that they were."

Joe held up a hand. "There is a little-known story written in ancient Akkadian called *Ana Harrani Sa Alaktasa La Tarat*, which translates roughly into *The Road Whose Course Does Not Turn Back*. I discovered it in the ruins of the city of Elba, located in what we now refer to as Syria. This story was only one of thousands that we found, all of which were completely intact! I remember finding this one of particular interest at the time, but due to the vastness of the discovery, I had quickly forgotten about it until Horace told me about these women.

"*Harrani* is a story about a high priestess who traveled throughout the world in search of knowledge. The god Anu gave her the power to travel through time. She journeyed to the past to meet holy figures, wise men, kings and queens, and all sorts of other godly messengers. After she had collected all the knowledge of the world and could speak in every tongue, she left the earth and joined the immortals."

"Joe, is it possible to get a copy of the complete translation?" asked Elaine.

Joe nodded and began pacing in front of the fireplace again. "It's at the museum and has been studied by both archeologists and anthropologists, but only as it pertains to its age and how it functioned in the culture of the time. Any research about the reality that inspired the story was discounted."

"As usual," Elaine groaned, shaking her head in disgust.

The chiming of the clock announced that it was 8:00 a.m., and everyone stood abruptly, having forgotten everything else until that moment. Only Melinda and Felix stayed where they were—Melinda because she had fallen asleep on the center sofa, and Felix who stared unblinkingly at the cold firebox, hardly seeming to hear the hurried goodbyes of the rest of the household. James Mulligan laid a hand on Felix's shoulder as he rushed to get dressed for the day, and Harmony called back from the doorway that Felix needn't worry about his missing classes, as she was sure he was exhausted.

"I'm sorry I didn't help you before," Elaine said, patting Felix on the head on her way out. "As soon as Joe gets me that story, I promise no matter what else is on my desk, that will come first."

When everyone else had gone, Joe sat down across from Felix and sighed. "I can have the people at the museum take a look at Bes. They're the best in the world when it comes to repairing antiquities."

Felix looked up and smiled absently. "If Indigo is the same person as the three others, then she might come back as someone else, right?"

Joe shrugged. "I suppose—we'll have to wait and see. But even if she does, it might be fifteen years, or then again it might be only a few months."

Felix cradled his chin in his hands, leaning forward to rest his elbows on his knees. "If they're all the same person, why did they all come to meet Stumpworthy? What made him so special that each one had to find him? Even Indigo had a connection to him. Now that he's gone, do you think she'll still come back?"

"Once again, it's a mystery to me," Joe said through a yawn.

Felix looked briefly over at Melinda, who was curled up in the tight knot. "You said earlier that something happened to Courtney that hadn't happened to the others. Did you remember what it was?"

Joe looked uneasy for a second before answering. "Millicent and Helen simply disappeared from Horace's life; he never knew what happened to them. He analyzed everything he could remember about the days and weeks before they vanished to see if there was a common thread, but when he couldn't find one, he took to following Courtney, disguised as an animal she wouldn't notice. One evening, as she was crossing the street in front of her apartment, he saw a truck travelling very fast, coming right toward her. He tried to warn her to get out of the way, but he was flying above her, a pigeon. Who knows what she understood from him in that form, but for whatever reason she stopped right in the middle of the road and stared directly up at him. The truck couldn't miss her."

CHAPTER NINETEEN

Felix could not believe what he was seeing. Across the street, Indigo was walking along as if she didn't have a care in the world. She was right in front of the *patisserie* near her building. He called to her but she seemed not to hear him. She was walking briskly, and he tried to catch up with her but he couldn't seem to cross the street; every time he tried, a car or a bus sped by. He called again. At last she heard him, stopped and smiled, and then without turning to check for traffic she stepped off the curb, right in front of a speeding bus.

Felix sat bolt upright, his eyes adjusting to the darkness of his room, his heart racing harder than he ever remembered for a dream.

The next afternoon Joe handed the translation of *Harrani* to Felix as he was preparing to leave for school. "Are you sure you wouldn't like your mum to analyze this before you try to read through it? I'm sure she will be able to fashion it into a more understandable form."

Felix took hold of the book and shook his head. "I'm sure I can manage. I have a couple of free periods today; I'll read through it and we can discuss it tonight." He opened the cover and began reading the first page. He grimaced as he struggled to make sense of the rambling lines and nonsense grammar, then reluctantly handed the manuscript back to Joe.

"I warned you," Joe said. "A direct translation from ancient Sumerian into English is not easy to read because it doesn't flow in the way we are accustomed to—and, quite frankly, it often doesn't make a lot of sense at first glance." Joe turned and walked toward the staircase. "On the upside, though, your mum's an expert at working with ancient texts, plus she'll be able to tell us if this little story is actually reality in disguise." Joe climbed up the stairs toward Elaine's office.

"But that usually takes a long time. What about Indigo? We need answers now."

Joe stopped and turned back to face Felix. "If Horace's experience gives us any hint of when we might see Indigo again, I think we have more time than we need."

Professor Mulligan hurried into the headmaster's office, skidding to a halt when he opened the door and saw Professor Horace Stumpworthy sitting behind his desk.

"Hello, James," Stumpworthy greeted kindly. "Do come in, and please shut the door behind you."

Mulligan's hand shook violently as he grabbed hold of the door handle. His fat body quivered, and his shirt was instantly saturated by what felt like a gallon of sweat oozing out of his pores. He wanted to run the other way, or at least scream out for help, but he did as he was told, clicking the door shut behind him.

Stumpworthy's head dropped forward as he slumped back into the chair. "I can tell from your expression that you thought I was really *him*," Felix's voice bragged from Horace's mouth. "I wanted to make sure I could still do this."

Mulligan staggered over to the chair facing the desk and collapsed onto it.

"Did I sound like him? It's been a long time since I've needed to." Mulligan nodded, and Felix scrunched Horace's face into a goofy grin, which made him look like a caricature of the real man. "I remembered what you said—that I should help you more, like at board meetings."

Mulligan dabbed the sweat off his forehead with a handkerchief and nodded. "You could have told me about this at home—or did you feel it more appropriate to give me a heart attack?"

"I wanted to make sure I could still fool you, because that means I could fool anyone else who might have known him. It's different when I go to the bank, because no one really knew him there, but here at the school…well, that's a different matter."

Professor Mulligan raised his hands in surrender. "I appreciate your help and I will let you know when I need it, but for now you are welcome to change back into your own body and get back to class."

Felix shook his head. "I have a couple of free periods, so I thought I would stay this way until I need to run. In fact, I've been doing some thinking: people might be getting suspicious because they never see the headmaster around. I think it would be good for the school to see him on a daily basis, at least for a while."

Felix left Mulligan still mopping sweat off his face and neck and walked down the hall toward Harmony's office. He knew she would be finishing her last class in minutes and couldn't resist surprising her.

"Good afternoon, Professor," a ginger-haired girl, who Felix only vaguely recognized, greeted him. "Have you been away? We haven't seen you much lately."

Felix felt the color drain from his face as he tried to maintain Stumpworthy's stalwart composure. "I'm always running in and out, in and out—always meetings to attend." He spoke quickly, lengthening his stride to get away as fast as possible.

Within two steps a short, wiry boy of about sixteen, with frizzy black hair and thick black-framed glasses, and a tall, thin girl the same age with a bob of icy-blond hair appeared around the corner, headed his way. Felix recognized them as the Rodent and the Ice Queen—nicknames Indigo had given them, for obvious reasons. "Professor Stumpworthy," the boy called. "Have the teams been chosen to represent the school in the European Science School Challenge in Germany this year? If not, I'd hope to be considered—I don't think anyone has more knowledge about slime molds and spore fungus than I."

Felix felt the hairs on the back of his neck bristle. "Yes, I understand that you did very well on your exam," he said dryly, "but didn't Felix Hutton do just as well?"

"Are you considering sending Felix to the competition?" the boy asked with a slight edge to his voice.

"He is one of our best students," Felix said proudly.

"I agree he's a clever kid—but, Professor, he's only fourteen, and the competition is for sixteen and older. Won't that be against the rules?"

Felix didn't respond immediately, embarrassed at being caught off guard and wondering if he'd just give himself away if he spent too long in this form. He looked quickly at his hands to make sure that they were still the professor's. "Of course it's against the rules. I…ah…just wanted to point out that many of our students are doing extremely well, and I'm sure the committee will decide who best represents the school in each category. Now, if you'll excuse me," he added hastily, "I have to meet with…"

"Just a minute, Professor Stumpworthy," Madame Rousseau demanded as she walked up behind them. "As you know, I am on that particular committee, and I want to know what protocol we are following this year. As you recall, at the end of last year's competition, all the rules were changed, with the top schools awarded a lot more flexibility. Have you given any thought as to how we will proceed, especially in light of the fact that we will be hosting the competition next year?"

Felix stared at her shock of gray hair standing on end for exactly ten seconds before answering. "I have a meeting to get to—in fact, I'm already late." He spat the words out in rapid succession while legging it down the hallway. "I promise to bring this up with Mulligan…that is, I mean James…what I mean to say is, I will talk with Professor Mulligan," he mumbled over his shoulder as he rounded the corner then disappeared into Harmony's office.

Harmony was furiously writing when he walked in. "What can I do for you, Felix?" she asked without looking up.

Felix smiled slyly and cleared his throat.

Harmony looked up from her papers and sat back. "Well, well, well—what do we have here? What possessed you to change into *him* today?"

Felix deflated and quickly examined his hands again. They were still those of Stumpworthy, so he ran his hands over his face, just in case part of him had transformed back into his fourteen-year-old self. When he felt the stubble of a beard, he knew something else must have gone wrong. "How did you know it was me?" he asked, walking to the windows to inspect his reflection.

Harmony offered an annoyed grin. "I sensed it was you when you walked in," she said, clicking her tongue. "I may not have transformation abilities, but I do have animal senses. Now are you going to tell me what's going on?"

Felix started to tell her exactly what he had told Professor Mulligan, but knew it was pointless to lie. "If Indigo is the same person Stumpworthy met all those years ago, then she's likely to come back. And each time she does, she connects with him."

"Indigo has only been gone a week. And from what you and Joe told us the other night, if she *is* going to return as someone else, she may not come back for years."

The door opened abruptly and James Mulligan barged in, shutting it quietly behind him. "Great," he whispered, a little out of breath. "I'm glad I found you, Felix. I had thought I wouldn't need you so soon, but I had forgotten, and you know how these things happen." Harmony motioned the professor to hurry up his explanation. Mulligan mopped his brow with one hand. "We have a brilliant new student arriving next week. This student is the brightest I've seen in some time. Can you imagine: a perfect entrance exam! I can't believe it had slipped my mind when you were in my office earlier. As you know, Professor Stumpworthy often greets exceptional students to personally offer our acceptance to the student and their family, and I think in this case it would be most appropriate. Since you were keen to masquerade as Professor Stumpworthy, I thought it would be perfect to do so again next week. Her name is Nichole—Nichole Renault. Her parents are unable to attend—traveling in Mongolia, or was it Mozambique?" His forehead wrinkled and he looked almost in pain, as if trying to squeeze the memory out of his brain. "Marrakesh? Well, somewhere exotic, anyway—something to do with their work, I imagine. But no matter. I know that Nichole will be thrilled to meet you—er—that is, Professor Stumpworthy.

In fact, in her letter she said how excited she was to have received your—I mean, the professor's invitation."

CHAPTER TWENTY

Felix had rehearsed his speech to welcome Nichole Renault to the school at least a hundred times, but when he looked at the dazzling blond-haired, blue-eyed beauty waiting in the reception area of the headmaster's office, he almost forgot his own name.

"Good afternoon, Professor Stumpworthy," she greeted graciously in perfect English with only a trace of a French accent.

"Nichole," he twittered after a few seconds, feeling the heat rise to his cheeks at the sound of his squeaking voice. He knew his face was rapidly approaching the color of a sunburnt raspberry, so he hurried across the room, leaving Nichole looking bewildered behind him.

"Please come in," James Mulligan said smoothly, guiding Nichole into the office as if there was nothing unusual about Professor Stumpworthy's behavior. "Dr. Melpot will be along in a minute. As the head of the science faculty, she'll be able to answer any questions you might have about our curriculum."

Felix took a deep breath when he reached the desk, ordering himself to stop acting like a child. Calmly, he turned to face Nichole and Professor Mulligan in the doorway, motioning to the chairs facing him with only the slightest tremor in his hand. Then, in a controlled and perfectly measured Stumpworthy voice, he said, "Nichole, please make yourself comfortable. We are so pleased you have decided to attend our school," he recited eloquently, and managed to repeat the rest of his ten-minute speech without hesitation or error. When he finished, he smiled and, just as he had rehearsed earlier, asked, "Tell me, Nichole: besides science, what are your other interests?"

He listened as she explained that she was an only child and didn't see much of her parents because they traveled frequently. His palms began to feel clammy when she mentioned she had always lived in Paris and had never left the city, even for a holiday. His pulse raced when she noted that in addition to science she found history exciting. And he almost lost his breath when she explained her interest in studying languages.

"My goal is to master as many of the world's languages as I can in my life," she said with pride. "So far I am fluent in eight, including Mandarin and Swahili."

Ten minutes after Nichole had left with James Mulligan on a guided tour of the school, Felix, who was back in his own body, flew out of Stumpworthy's office and made a beeline for Harmony's.

"Sorry I couldn't make the meeting with the new girl," Harmony said, not looking up from the papers she was marking on her desk. "There was an explosion in the chemistry lab— nothing serious, but I had to calm the situation. What a mess! Luckily it wasn't a toxic blast, but it may take a week or two for Charlie Huntsley to scrub the stuff off his hands and face." She looked up with a wry smile. "He's not in any danger; the substance is a combination of dipertenes and tripertenes, which, as you know, is simply tree pitch. But he had thrown in some other chemicals that made it explosive, as well as making it about a hundred times thicker and, unfortunately for Charlie, stickier than it would normally be. It wouldn't be so bad if it wasn't green—it makes him look a bit like a swamp monster."

"It's her! Nichole is Indigo," Felix railed, not caring for the moment about the chemistry lab or the green globs sticking to Charlie Huntsley's face. "I have never been so certain of anything in my life!"

Harmony glanced down at stack of papers that she had been marking. Suddenly they held little importance. She put down her pen and looked back at Felix with an intense gaze. "What do we do now?"

Relieved that she seemed to believe him, Felix shook his head. "I have no idea. But I'm not losing her again—not before we figure this out."

Dusk's arrival bathed everything in a dusty haze as Felix bounded up the steps to the front door of the mansion, ready to take on anything Melinda might have morphed herself into. Nothing she could do would bother him today. He was still buzzing from the encounter with Indigo—well, Nichole—and couldn't wait to tell everyone about it as soon as possible. He reached eagerly for the door but hadn't even touched the handle yet when it swung open, causing him to lose his balance and collide with Dr. Zhang, who was on his way out in a rush.

"Felix," Dr. Zhang said in a soft voice. "We were just leaving." He then turned and settled a hand on the shoulder of a giggling little girl who stood at his side. Her eyes twinkled out of her pixie-like face, and two long black ponytails hung over her shoulders. "I would like to introduce you to my granddaughter, Ming Su," he said. The little girl thrust her hand out to shake Felix's.

"I'm six," she said, her English carrying a sharp American accent. "'You can call me Min Min. That's my favorite book—*The Dreams of Min Min*. I'm just like her because I travel to the underworld when I dream, too. I've met lots of dead people—Roman emperors and princes and movie stars. Melinda said she has cool dreams too." Felix smiled reluctantly as he shook her tiny hand, surprised at the firmness of her grip.

"My granddaughter has a very active imagination," Dr. Zhang said, turning to look down at Ming Su. "Min Min, we must be on our way; there is more work to be done with those who are still living." Then, as if on a mission of the utmost urgency, Dr. Zhang and Ming Su galloped down the front steps.

"What was he doing here so late?" Felix asked a few minutes later when he found Melinda reading in the library.

"Dr. Zhang's granddaughter wanted a book he'd lent me about this girl…"

"Who visits dead people—I know."

"But only in her dreams," Melinda added ominously. "Kind of makes you wonder if it's just a story, if you know what I mean."

Felix did, but didn't feel like discussing it now.

"They also invited me to go to the Chinese Garden festival with them this weekend, since it was cancelled a few weeks ago due to the rain."

Felix didn't remember and didn't care. "Did you see anything in his eyes this time?"

"Nope, just normal human reflections. I'm starting to wonder if I imagined what I saw before. Do you think I dreamt about the images?"

Felix readjusted his glasses that had slipped down to end of his nose. "I was there, remember? If you dreamt about it, then you did it while you were awake." He walked across the room and dropped his schoolwork on the desk. "This all just adds to the mystery," he said in an ominous tone. "What were the images you saw? Why did you see them in the first place, and why didn't you see them today? And the big question: who is this Dr. Zhang" He looked over the top of his glasses, which had slipped down to the tip of his nose again, and tried to focus on the blurred image of his sister. "But frankly, I don't want to talk about him right now," he said as he crossed the room to stand triumphantly in front her. "Indigo has returned! This time as a girl named Nichole. It's just like in Stumpworthy's diary."

As Felix explained about Nichole, Melinda rocked her head back against the sofa and stared up at the domed glass ceiling that loomed three stories above them. "You said she hasn't met you, as you, yet. What are you going to do if she recognizes you?"

Felix's smile flattened. "I've been assigned as her buddy, to help her until she gets settled in, so I guess I'll find out tomorrow."

"So if she does recognize you, are you going to ask her what she is?"

"Are you crazy? She wouldn't tell me anything, just like I wouldn't tell anyone that I'm an Athenite."

"You would tell them if they already knew."

"But I don't know what she is," Felix said in a defeated voice. "I can't very well go up to her, accuse her of not being human, and ask for details."

Melinda didn't see why not, but she let it drop anyway. "Even if she doesn't know you, do you think she remembers being Indigo, or those other people? Or maybe she doesn't know anything about her other lives and is totally into her new identity." Melinda's voice was excited, while Felix's smile melted into a frown. "You should talk to her about Indigo just to see what kind of reaction she has."

Felix gave her a blank look. "It would be nice if she said, 'Yeah, I'm Indigo' and then told me everything about herself, but I don't think that's going to happen. I wish we knew what we were dealing with, or even who. All we do know is that she's bound to disappear again, and we don't know when or why."

"At least we know that she always comes back. *Shu gao qian zhang ye luo gui gen.*"

Pressure was building in Felix's temples. "No more Chinese stories—every time we start talking about Indigo, YOU start spouting gibberish."

"It's a proverb, not a story, and it means *even if a tree reaches the height of ten thousand feet, falling leaves return to their roots.* Or in other words, people always return to where they came from. They've been saying it for thousands of years in China."

"We're not in China," Felix said, exasperated. "Indigo was not Chinese; Nichole is not Chinese."

Melinda shook her head as if pitying him. "Whether a person is or isn't Chinese has nothing to do with it. Millicent disappeared and came back as Helen, Helen came back as Courtney, Courtney came back as Indigo and now Indigo is Nichole. Whatever form she takes, she always comes back to Paris and she always reconnects with Stumpworthy. It's like she's a spirit with unfinished business."

"Unfinished business," Felix mused, his headache easing slightly. "That's the first thing you've said that makes any kind of sense."

CHAPTER TWENTY-ONE

Felix entered the school the next day with the weight of dread on his shoulders. It was a far cry from the enthusiasm he had felt only the day before. He walked into the admissions office with the glow of perspiration on his face, causing his glasses to slip down his pointed nose no matter how many times he pushed them back in place.

Nichole, who had been waiting for at least half an hour, smiled when he walked in. "I am pleased to meet you, Felix," she said formally, flashing the most brilliantly white teeth Felix had ever seen. "Please forgive my forwardness, but I feel as if I already know you. Have we met before?"

Felix felt dizzy as his mind raced with possible answers, none of which sounded terribly good at the moment. Should he say, "Of course, when you were Indigo," or "Yes, when I was Stumpworthy"? He opened his mouth three times without making a sound, then finally croaked the word "I" just as the class bell rang. "Saved by the bell," he whispered, his cheeks reddening partly from the cliché—then, in a louder voice to be heard over the clanging, "We only have three minutes to get to general science, and Madame Rousseau doesn't appreciate tardiness."

They hurried down the hallway, past the turning heads of every other student they met. The ginger-haired girl who had talked to Felix while he was masquerading as Stumpworthy collided with a sandy-haired boy of about the same age, all because she couldn't take her eyes off Nichole. Charlie Huntsley, whose face was still splotched with green goo, ran straight into a locker door left open by the Rodent. Even he seemed mesmerized by Nichole's beauty, much to the obvious chagrin of the Ice Queen, who glared first at Nichole and then her constant companion. Felix smiled for the first time that day. Each student they passed looked at Nichole as if watching a movie star glide by—a movie star that just happened to be with him.

They made it to class with barely enough time to take their seats, Felix in the front row and Nichole three rows behind him: the same seat Indigo had occupied a few weeks earlier.

All eyes focused on the board at the front of the class, where the word *Hirudotherapy* was scrawled in chalk. Madame Rousseau marched into the classroom and took her place at the lectern.

"*Hirudotherapy*," she said with her characteristic sharp emphasis, "refers to the use of leeches in medicine. They were used throughout the centuries, from Ancient Egypt to Medieval Europe to more modern civilizations. They were considered a cure-all in ancient times and were used to treat anything from knife wounds to measles. It was believed that these parasitic creatures would suck out the toxins that inflicted the patient. Was it barbaric or simply ahead of its time? Today we are going to discuss the real benefits of using leeches in medical treatment and explore the methods in which doctors still employ them."

After the bell rang, Felix waited for Nichole in the hallway while she tried to wriggle out of new-girl questions from almost all their classmates. By the time she joined him, they only had two minutes before mathematics was due to begin. Once again they hurried along the hall to the exact same reception. Felix couldn't help enjoying being at— well, near—the center of so much awe and attention. By the time they left mathematics, though, Felix was feeling a bit stifled by Nichole's otherworldly draw. Even people who had paused to gawk at her before did so again. For the first time, Felix realized Nichole seemed to be enjoying her celebrity status; in fact, she was paying far more attention to the people who took notice of her than she was to him. Instead of swelling with pride at being her companion, Felix was beginning to feel invisible.

At lunch, Felix left Nichole to fend for herself in the cafeteria, seeing as at least three boys were happy to help her find a seat and four others argued over who would bring her lunch. She didn't seem at all bothered when he left her with her new array of fans, and as he exited the cafeteria, he wondered if she had even noticed he was gone.

He walked down the hallway with a hollow feeling, wondering if his relationship with Indigo had disappeared along with that form. He was so absorbed in his feeling of emptiness that he didn't notice the little ginger-haired girl in front of him until she shrieked. He stared at her for a second, then looked around the corridor to see what the trouble might be, but they were alone. He smiled sheepishly at the terrified girl.

"What's the problem?" he asked as kindly as he could, only to have her scream again, then turn and run at top speed down the hallway. Felix reached up to adjust his glasses, thinking the feeling of dread that had accompanied him to school that morning was obviously a predictor of his day, but he stopped dead when he realized he could see through his hand. He jerked his left arm up to stare at where his other hand should have been, only to confirm that it simply wasn't there.

"Felix, why aren't you in class?" Harmony asked as she pushed her office door open with her back; her arms were laden with books. "No problems with the new Indigo, I hope," she said under her breath, kicking the door shut as she turned toward her desk and saw what little there was to see of Felix. "What do you think you're doing? I admit becoming invisible, or even partially invisible, is a neat trick, but it's not appropriate for school."

"I didn't do it intentionally," groaned Felix. "It just happened. I was feeling—well, you know, invisible, because that's how Nichole treated me, and then somehow I was. The problem is, I can't undo it."

Harmony dropped the books onto her desk and walked around to where Felix was standing. "It would have been better if you'd vanished completely. That way you could still walk around the school and no one would be the wiser—that is, if you got rid of the clothes first. As it is, you just look like you're made out of see-through gelatin, and that, my friend, is just a little more difficult to get away with."

"That's why I'm in here," Felix snapped. Harmony nodded and walked back around her desk.

"I hope nobody has seen you."

"Only this ginger-haired girl: loads of freckles, always wears her hair in about fifteen plaits all over her head," he said, holding his hand up to his shoulder.

"That must have been Nikki Pinksky…smart girl, but a bit of a storyteller." Harmony looked at Felix's watery form and shook her head. "Poor child—no one will believe her about this, and for once she will be telling the absolute truth." She sat down at her desk and leaned forward on her elbows. "Tell me what exactly Indigo did to force you into this state."

"Remember, she isn't Indigo anymore; her name is Nichole, and she really didn't *do* anything except ignore me."

"But you used to be so close. Why do you think she's so different this time?"

"That's why: because *she* is totally different and I don't know if I really care for the person she has become this time. But I suppose it doesn't really matter how I feel about her—she's not here because of me, she's here because of Stumpworthy."

"You're probably right, and we'll figure out what to do about that later. Right now, you have to either disappear completely or change back so we can get you out of here."

Felix closed his eyes and tried to focus on being himself again. He felt the tingle of transformation begin almost immediately, then wane as his thoughts darted between his experience with Nichole and his feelings about Indigo, and then to the man who was important to both of them. With greater concentration he tried again, but he couldn't keep his mind focused. He opened his eyes, sighed in resignation, then reluctantly decided to give in to his brain's obvious desire. He shut his eyes again and within seconds had completed his transformation. Shifting uncomfortably in his seat, he opened his eyes and examined his hands, which were no longer transparent but were definitely not his.

CHAPTER TWENTY-TWO

James Mulligan knocked on Harmony's office door three times, barging in before she had a chance to invite him. "Harmony," he barked urgently, then stopped abruptly when he saw that she wasn't alone. "You should have told me you were busy."

"I might have if you had given me the chance," Harmony said in a stern tone. "Now that you're here, please come in and say hello to an old friend."

Mulligan clicked the door shut and waddled over to Felix, his hand outstretched. "I didn't mean to interrupt a reunion. I am James Mulligan, and you are?"

"Uncanny," Harmony chuckled. "You really don't recognize Indigo. I had thought seeing her would jog your memory."

Mulligan backed away immediately as if he might contract dengue fever, or worse, from the girl sitting in front of him. "I can honestly say that I don't," he said, beads of sweat building on his forehead.

"You can relax," Felix's voice sighed out of Indigo's mouth. "It's only me, not her."

Mulligan staggered backward until he bumped into Harmony's desk. "My boy, what have you done to yourself? I don't know if this is a relief or not." He looked over at Harmony with a bewildered gaze. "The only thing I know about Indigo is what you have told me. Intellectually, the whole thing made some strange kind of sense before... but now! I feel like an amnesiac, which I must say is a most peculiar feeling." He looked at Felix and shook his head. "I know you are involved in sorting out the mystery surrounding her disappearance, but why, in Heaven's name, would you want to change into her?"

"I didn't want to," Felix snarled, standing up and walking toward the door. "I didn't seem to have much choice. Harmony can explain everything, because right now all I want to do is to get out of here and go home."

"Felix, I don't think that's wise. Someone might see you...I'm mean Indigo."

Felix turned back briefly. "If Professor Mulligan's reaction is any indication, then I don't think I have to worry about being recognized."

Felix left Harmony's office in Indigo's guise only seconds before the bell rang. His pulse raced when the clanging began, bracing himself as doors swung open and a stampede of students spilled out into hallway. No one took any notice of the tall, auburn-haired girl as they raced to their next class, Nikki Pinksky even slamming right into her. Felix's throat tightened at the wide-eyed stare frozen on Nikki's pale face before she managed to push around him and continue down the hallway without so much as an "excuse me"—unusual behavior for a girl who always seemed to be smiling and was never at a loss for words.

After that encounter, people seemed to look right through the girl that, only weeks before, had walked to class down this very hallway. The Rodent and the Ice Queen strutted by without even a glance and Charley Huntsley, who Felix had always imagined fancied Indigo, didn't say a word as they passed. None of the people who had listened to Indigo's speeches in mathematics on intrinsic values and parabolic equations said hello, and none of the hundreds of people who had applauded when she received the Gold Award nodded or waved or acknowledged her in anyway. Absently he looked at Indigo's hands to confirm that he hadn't dissolved into nothingness. He had not.

He reached his locker, pausing only briefly to watch the last of the students disappear into their classrooms as he fiddled with his lock.

"Excuse me," Nichole said, clearing her throat. Felix jumped and slammed his shoulder into his locker. "Sorry, I didn't mean to startle you," she added politely. "I'm looking for Felix Hutton. Do you know where I can find him?"

Felix extricated himself from the locker, dropping his chemistry book on the floor in the process, and turned around to face her. His heart pounded uncomfortably as he braced himself for her reaction, smiling shyly when he met her eyes.

Nichole apparently didn't recognize her former self, turning nonchalantly to survey the hallway while she continued, "This is his locker, isn't it?" Felix nodded silently, too terrified to answer having never practiced Indigo's voice before. "He was meant to show me around today," Nichole huffed, resting her gaze on Indigo's face, "but I haven't seen him since before lunch, and he has my class schedule." When Felix only shrugged in reply, Nichole rolled her eyes and made like she had intended to leave, but at the last moment she hesitated, cocking her head to one side. "Wait a minute," she said in an accusing tone. "You look familiar; have we met before?"

Felix jerked his head from side to side, then spun around to face his locker. "I have to get to class," he announced in an exaggeratedly high-pitched voice.

"I'll go with you." Nichole added, "Maybe that's where I'm meant to be."

"No, no. It's not," Felix insisted frantically, spinning back to face her. "I have an…um…ah…a private class." He slammed his locker shut, then squeezed by Nichole. "You should ask at the office," he offered while legging it down the hallway. "They should know where you're meant to be."

Felix hurried up the front steps to the mansion hoping that no one would see him, especially not Melinda. During the bus ride home, he had succeeded in partially transforming, but he was uncertain about the results. He knew from the feel of his face that it belonged to him. His long, pointed nose and sharp chin was unmistakably his, as were his eyes—

since forgetting his glasses in Harmony's office, the world had become hazy and out of focus. However, not all of his features had returned to normal. Indigo's hair still topped his head, and his hands were not visible at all.

He opened the door as quietly as its squeaking hinges would allow and squeezed in through the narrow opening. The foyer was deserted, the house was so quiet it appeared no one was home, but Felix knew better that to trust his eyes and ears alone. He closed his eyes and concentrated to detect if anyone was around, finally feeling the presence of someone down the hallway toward the library. He crept across the marble floor, then tiptoed up the sweeping staircase, never taking his eyes off the hallway that led to the library.

"Felix?" Elaine gasped above him on the stairs. "What have you done to yourself?"

As the color drained from his face, he felt Melinda's presence at his shoulder. "Don't say a word," he begged. "You can't believe the day that I've had."

"You can explain later," Elaine said firmly as she hooked her arm through his and dragged him back down the stairs. "Right now I want you to come to the library. I have the translation of *Ana Harrani Sa Alaktasa La Tarat*."

"From now on we'll refer to the story only as *Harrani*, which means *road*," Elaine began, courageously stifling a laugh when her eyes fell on Felix. "Could you at least do something about that?" she asked, pointing to his long hair and his invisible hands that were fumbling with a pencil. "It's very distracting."

Felix shook his head, "'I've been trying, but I can't concentrate right now—can you just tell us about the story?"

Elaine nodded and began pacing in front of the sofa where Felix sat uncomfortably next to Melinda, who couldn't stop staring at him, finding it impossible not to grin. "There's not a lot of difference to what Joe told us: the story is about a woman—a high priestess named Delondra—who was given powers by the god Anu to travel through time and around the world in search of knowledge. What wasn't obvious in the first translation is that this woman changed her appearance with each new place and time she traveled to. She was always a human female, but on one occasion she was a tall dark woman with black hair worn in intricate plaits, the next time she had hair the color of the sun that danced in the wind like serpents, and so on."

"Sounds familiar," Felix said. "Nichole doesn't look anything like Indigo, and from what little I read in Stumpworthy's diary, the others didn't look alike either."

"Exactly," Elaine continued. "And because the first translation was a broad explanation of the story, it didn't take into account another important element that might relate to Indigo—and, I assume, all of the others. During her travels on Earth, she had no knowledge about her past journeys or her past experiences. While she maintained the knowledge from her experiences, she didn't know how she came to possess such knowledge. In the end, after she had collected all the knowledge of the world, she traveled to an island where she lived as an immortal."

"Like Paradise Shore," Melinda asked excitedly.

"I suppose so—after all, this story was written in the same part of the world at around the same time. It was common to use parts of stories to tell new ones, changing elements to suit different audiences."

Felix smoothed his hands through Indigo's long hair and said softly, "She traveled through time to gather knowledge, and until she had gathered enough, you could say *that* was her unfinished business." He squinted in a failed attempt to get his mother into focus. "When did she complete her travels? How did she know when she had collected all she needed?"

Elaine shrugged. "In the story, Anu decided when she had completed her task."

Felix massaged his chin with his invisible thumb and index finger as if stroking a goatee. "Did the story have any other characters that seemed important, like Stumpworthy seems to be to Indigo?"

"I don't recall a specific person, but animals seemed important. That's not unusual for stories of this era, because animals were integral in all aspects of life." Elaine handed Felix several typed pages. "This is the translation; you can read it and see what you think. Maybe there's something I've overlooked."

CHAPTER TWENTY-THREE

It had taken about an hour for Felix to transform completely back into himself. He was left in a state of physical exhaustion, but his mind was completely awake, darting from one thought to the next. Now seated at his desk, surrounded by books on Sumerian mythology and time travel, he poured through a magazine called *Reincarnation Monthly*, while Melinda, seated comfortably on the sofa facing the fireplace, finished reading the story about *Harrani*.

"You're not going to believe this," she said in awe. "This story reminds me of *The Dreams of Min Min*."

Felix looked over his glasses at her. "That doesn't surprise me—these days, everything reminds you of something Chinese."

Melinda ignored his sarcasm. "In *Harrani*, Delondra traveled back in time to gain knowledge by meeting famous people. In *The Dreams of Min Min*, she traveled to the Underworld to meet dead people." Melinda read Felix's thoughts and the smug expression on his face. "I know you think I'm crazy, but I'm not," she snorted before he could say a word. "Their goals were the same—to gain knowledge by visiting people from the past."

The smugness gradually faded and Felix nodded seriously. "You may be on to something. Are there other similarities?"

"Lots of animals."

Felix leaned forward onto his elbows. "It could be a coincidence: as Mum said, animals were always in stories."

Melinda shook her head as a frown creased her brow. "I know that, but I think there's something more important about them. I just don't know what it is."

When Indigo walked out of the school hand in hand with a tiger named Min Min after announcing they were on their way to meet Henry the Eighth, Felix gave up on trying to sleep. It was the third dream about Indigo that night. Noticing that it was almost 6 a.m. already, he groaned and got out of bed.

The rest of the morning disappeared into a blur and he found himself in the crowded hallway at school, standing in front of his locker feeling that perhaps the last twenty-four hours hadn't happened at all.

"Felix," Nichole called from behind him, bringing him instantly into the present. "I heard you weren't feeling yourself yesterday."

For once the heat didn't rise to his cheeks when he met her eyes; he found himself feeling surprisingly calm in her presence. "I'm fine now. Sorry about taking your class schedule with me."

She stared at him for an uncomfortably long time. "I found my way around in the end. I asked this girl who was at your locker where you were, but she wasn't very helpful."

Felix tried his best to look puzzled, bringing his eyebrows as close together as possible. "That's strange. I wonder who that could have been. Do you remember what she looked like?"

Nichole opened her mouth to answer, then shook her head. "That's the funniest thing. I usually never forget a face, but for the life of me, I cannot remember hers."

Felix tried in vain to quash the smile that curled the corners of his mouth. "Maybe you'll remember if you see her again. Was there anything distinctive about her?"

"Nothing…absolutely nothing. I remember thinking at the time that I had met her before…I was convinced I had. Now I can't remember anything about her. How weird is that?" She shook her head, throwing her shimmering blond hair over her shoulders. "I should be getting used to forgetting things—I have so much in my head all the time that I sometimes forget how it got there."

Felix had the urge to tell her all about herself—to tell her about Indigo and the others; to tell her about her reincarnations that had given her incredible knowledge. But he only smiled and nodded. "Yeah, sometimes I forget stuff, too."

The computer screen was illuminated with the words:

DREAMS OF MIN MIN
Author: unknown.
Origin: China.
Written (circa): unknown.

The printer grumbled as it spit out the last page. Melinda gathered them all, tapping them on the desk to square the corners, then walked across the library to take her favorite place on the sofa and began reading.

Min Min rose up from her body, turning to watch herself sleep as she drifted across the room then glided effortlessly through the wall of the house and out into the moonlit garden. Her long black hair hung loosely across her shoulders and down her back. Her dark eyes were bright and glistened with the excitement that she had felt all day.

She was greeted by the serpent dragon Tianlong, the protector of the sky and the palaces of the Gods. He bent down and helped her climb onto his back, then lifted into the air in flight. They flew higher into the sky until the ground below had melted into only one color in the distance.

It was not long before the earth had disappeared completely into darkness as dense as the blackest calligrapher's ink. Tianlong continued on his upward journey until the sky lightened and the warmth of sunshine blanketed them. Beautiful green land became visible below them, surrounded by the deepest sapphire blue water Min Min had ever seen.

Sensing her question, Tianlong turned his enormous horned head so that she could hear him. "That is where we are going, to the land of your ancestors."

Melinda looked up and smiled. "They're going to an island," she whispered excitedly. "Just like Paradise Shore."

Excitedly, she continued to read about Min Min's travels to meet people who had died a long time before. Each time she left her sleeping body and glided through the wall of her house, she was met by an animal. After the dragon, a snake with ruby-colored eyes brought her to a faraway place where the famous third-century scholar Li Si greeted her. On her next adventure, a magnificent warhorse bore her to meet the famous scientist Ming Antu. Min Min met the historian Sima Qian after riding on the back of a goat, then walked hand in hand with a monkey who introduced her to Zhuge Liang, a great strategist of ancient times. One night she walked miles with a rooster on her shoulder to meet Emperor Han Wudi.

Night after night Min Min left her sleeping body to visit people from the past, each time guided by a different animal that Melinda finally recognized as the animals of the Chinese zodiac. A dog guided her to meet Kong Fuzi, whom Melinda recognized was none other than the famous philosopher Confucius; a pig carried her a distance of a hundred miles to listen to a song of the beautiful princess Wang Zhaojun; a rat led her to meet the writer Ban Jieyu; a tiger introduced her to the explorer Zheng He, who was the first person ever to travel around the globe, and finally a rabbit took her to meet Du Fu, the famous Chinese poet.

After her visit with Du Fu, Tianlong the dragon returned.

"It is time," he said firmly, to which Mm Min nodded solemnly. She climbed onto his back and they flew high into the sky just as they

had done before. They flew into the darkness, leaving the earth behind in blackness, then into the light that warmed them.

Tianlong turned his enormous head toward her.

"Do not be sad," she said when she looked into his sorrowful eyes. "1 know this is my last journey."

He nodded his head slightly, then looked down at the lovely green land below them. "It is time for you to join your ancestors."

Chapter Twenty-Four

Felix felt his mood disintegrate the moment he stepped into the mansion. He didn't know what had caused the change of humor, having enjoyed a carefree day with Nichole that had been reminiscent of the days when she was Indigo. Everything had felt somewhat normal; even her new appearance was becoming familiar. There was no doubt that she was different, and not just in the way that she looked. But Felix didn't care about the changes anymore; he didn't care because he had changed, too. The feelings he had held for Indigo were replaced by the comfort of a simple friendship with Nichole. It had been nice talking about science and sharing their interests in chemical formulas and mathematic equations, and Felix knew he didn't want more than that.

He shuffled down the hallway toward the library, eager to get started on the homework he had been assigned in chemistry, physics, and biology, but with each step he felt worse, a feeling of dread that gave him a piercing headache.

He paused at the entrance to the library and took a deep breath to bolster himself, then bravely walked inside. There, in the center of the room, lay an enormous tiger, with paws the size of dinner plates and a head at least as broad as a super-sized pizza. A throaty purr rumbled out of its humungous chest as it raised its head to take him in, making his heart pound uncomfortably. Rationally he knew it had to be Melinda inside that beast, but realistically he had never seen her manage such a perfect transformation.

The tiger stretched and pushed up to a sitting position as its face began melting, distorting its black and orange fur into a mass of beige; its eyes softened into a crystal blue hue and its mouth flattened into soft, pinkish lips. An instant later, Melinda's nose and freckled cheeks were clearly visible, forming one of the most bizarre pictures Felix had ever seen.

"Pretty good, right," she chattered surreally. "I've tried them all, but this is my best one."

Felix took a second to regain his composure, finding it difficult to look directly at her since she looked like she was being swallowed by a giant tiger. "What's all of them?" he finally managed as he dropped his books on his desk.

"The Chinese Zodiac," she said proudly.

"Just because you're home-schooled doesn't mean you get to play around transforming all day."

Melinda ignored him. "After I read *Min Min*, I had to try. I am getting really good at becoming almost anything I want, as long as I stay focused."

"Yeah, like that's going to happen," Felix said under his

breath; then, in a louder voice: "Did you find anything in *Min Min* that connects with *Harrani*?"

She nodded and stood up, flicking her tail as she began to pace in front of him. "As we already knew, both Min Min and Delondra searched for knowledge, and after rereading both stories, I now know the importance of the animals." She stopped and turned to face him. "They were the guides! In *Min Min*, animals of the Chinese zodiac took her to meet famous people from history, so I figured she probably went on journeys once a year for twelve years. On her thirteenth and last journey, she was met by her first guide again: the dragon. It's obvious animals were Delondra's guides too. When she went back in time, she rode on a donkey or elephant's back or was accompanied by a dog or cat." Melinda absently looked down at her tiger paws and smiled. "The stories also end the same way: they both go to an island."

Felix sat down at his desk and began sorting through his homework. "From what you've said, it makes me think they might be the same story, retold by merchants and explorers during their travels. They always did that kind of thing, and changed parts of the stories depending on their audience. So it's still hard to tell if they're just stories or if they really connect to Indigo and Nichole."

Melinda walked over to the desk, rose up onto her hind legs, and placed her giant front paws on top of Felix's work. "They both moved through time until their last journey, and on their last journey they left the world forever," she said in the most ominous tone she could manage.

Felix looked into her face, which seemed comically small compared to the enormity of the tiger's head. "You're wrinkling my papers."

Melinda lowered her head to within only a few centimeters of his face. "Don't you get it? If these stories are about real people like Indigo, then we know they don't travel forever. In the end they go away and, for the people they leave behind, it's like they die."

Felix stared at her and shook his head. "That might be true in these stories, but in real life, people don't remember them when they go—they simply don't exist anymore. Even Mulligan doesn't remember Indigo; no one does, except us." He cleared his throat and motioned toward his books, thinking he would prefer to do his homework than listen to any more of what Melinda had to say.

Having read his thoughts clearly, she pushed herself off the desk and walked over to the fireplace, where she sat in a regal pose with her back to the flames. The relaxing warmth felt incredible on her fur-covered back, sending her into a contemplative state. What was it about those stories that drew her in, giving her the sense that they weren't just stories? Why didn't Felix feel the same way? Why was it so difficult for him to see that Delondra and Min Min were the same type of people as Indigo and the women in Stumpworthy's diary?

It was this last thought that made Melinda's mind race, remembering the clue that seemed to link everything together. "The ghosts," she whispered only loud enough for herself to hear. "The ghostly images in their eyes that only

Athenites can see," she added excitedly. Then she recalled a proverb Dr. Zhang had mentioned on occasion, always with a private little smile. *The eyes are the windows of the soul.*

She jumped to her feet, not noticing until a searing pain raced up her back that she had swung her burnished tail right into the flames. "Felix, help me!" she shouted as the flames curled around the tip of her tail and the fur sizzled into acrid smoke.

Annoyed at her interruption, Felix looked over his glasses only to find her running in circles in front of the fire, her tail alight and smoking. Instantly he jumped up and grabbed a small rug from beside the couch.

"Hold still, let me smother it!" he yelled as he grabbed her lashing tail and wrapped it tightly in the rug. The flames died quickly, and he backed away from the overpowering smell of smoldering hair. "I hate to think about what that's going to feel like when you transform back," he said. "If I were you, I'd stay like that for a while—maybe put your tail in some ice water."

Melinda stared at him, ignoring for the moment the wisps of smoke, the burnt hair and the pain filtering into her senses. "Animals can see things that humans can't. Like seeing a soul through the eyes of another."

Felix loosed her tail and nervously adjusted his glasses. "I don't think you suffered any serious burns—it looks like the hair just got singed."

Melinda's expression didn't change. "Felix, listen to me," she begged. "The animals recognized Delondra and Min Min, and I think they did so by looking into their eyes! It's the same way Stumpworthy recognized the women—he saw the ghosts, just like I saw the ghosts in Indigo's eyes!"

"I know all that," Felix groaned.

"But what you don't seem to understand is that the animals in the stories must represent Athenites!"

Felix stared at her for a long moment, then nodded very slowly. "I suppose that would make sense—the way they used stories to explain what they couldn't understand."

"Exactly! And in order for them to understand people that traveled through time, they invented stories about high priestesses and gods and girls flying around in their dreams."

Felix cradled his chin as if deep in thought. "Okay, I can understand how the stories relate to the Indigos of the world and I can accept the fact that Athenites played a role from time to time, but I don't buy the rest. Remember, according to Joe, Courtney died, which would mean her journey had ended—and if that was the case, then how do you explain Indigo, and now Nichole?"

"Simple," Melinda quipped. "They must be different people. The women Stumpworthy connected with were probably the same *type* of person as Indigo, but not the *same person*."

Felix took on a thoughtful look. "You said in the stories, the animals were the guides that led Delondra and Min Min to meet important people. So if the animals are Athenites, how does this *guide* theory work? I know for a fact that Stumpworthy never did anything for Indigo—obviously less for Nichole. And the only people he ever introduced were Mulligan and Harmony and me."

Melinda smiled slyly. "That's because he's clearly not their guide. You are."

CHAPTER TWENTY-FIVE

The November sunshine was blindingly bright as it reflected off the tall white walls of the Chinese Garden. Nichole shielded her eyes behind dark sunglasses as she and Felix made their way up the street toward the entrance.

I can't believe I let Melinda talk me into this, Felix thought, recalling her insistence that he bring Nichole to the Garden's opening celebration so Melinda could look into her eyes, convinced she would see more than Indigo's ghosts. "This had better be worth it," he grumbled, hastily adding, "I still have about six more pages to write for biology."

"I finished my paper two days ago," Nichole stated impassively. "This makes for a nice change of pace. I find schoolwork so all-encompassing; I sometimes forget all about the outside world. To tell you the truth, if a place is not connected to my studies, it's likely I haven't been there. Obviously, visiting a Chinese garden is something I would never have done on my own."

Felix gave her a skeptical look. "That surprises me,

especially since you can speak Mandarin."

"I may speak the language, but I don't know anything about the culture. What I've learned about other countries has been through books, or from my parents' experiences."

The mention of Nichole's parents gave Felix a curious pause; he had never actually thought about her family. "Don't you ever travel with them?"

Nichole shook her head. "They travel and I study—that's the way it has always been and that's the way it will always be. It is very important to them that I complete my studies. I've never missed even one day of school. During holidays, I have extra tutoring and lessons to make sure I'm always at the top of my class."

Felix glanced at her stoic expression and wondered if she was really as nonchalant about that as she appeared. "Our family has lived all over the world because of my mum's work. My sister and I have seen some pretty amazing things."

"My life is very different from yours," Nichole said flatly. "I see my parents once a year, if that…I hardly know them, and I can't say I really care if I see them at all anymore. You probably can't understand that."

Felix couldn't. His family was different, to be sure, but he'd never imagined being apart from them for long periods of time. He recognized now, more than ever, that Nichole wasn't like him or anyone else he had ever known. All he knew about her was that she was some kind of time traveler and, as such, he surmised she must have time travelers for parents. He nervously reached up and adjusted his glasses, wondering if Nichole and her parents had a choice about their fate or if someone or something else controlled their journeys, sending them here or there, alone or together, as it pleased.

Nichole didn't notice the deepening lines arching their way across Felix's forehead. She was inspecting the tall white wall bordering their path, then looked across the street at the row of seventeenth-century buildings wedged tightly together, standing as islands in a sea of pavement. "I would never have guessed there was a garden behind these walls. This part of the city isn't exactly known for its greenery—there's not a blade of grass or a tree in sight."

Felix didn't respond, still lost in thought about where in time Nichole's parents might be, wondering when she saw them last or if she really ever did. "Do you talk to your parents when they travel?" he blurted out, wishing immediately that he hadn't.

"Not often," she said in the same flat tone. "Where they travel, modern communication isn't always available—I'm sure you can understand that."

"Yeah, I think I'm beginning to," Felix said knowingly as they passed through the tall wooden gates that marked the entrance to the garden.

They stopped when they reached a large paved courtyard surrounded by Chinese-style, tile-roofed buildings. A very large pond shimmered at the far end, spanned by three bridges leading to even more buildings and pathways. Tall water plants grew near the shoreline, and meticulously raked garden beds with sparse arrangements of plants trailed around the water's edge and alongside the buildings. Rocks of various sizes were strategically placed in each bed, looking like mountains jutting up from the flatness of a prairie.

Nichole looked around with a curious frown. "Are you sure this is the garden? I still don't see any grass, and I would hardly call those trees," she said, pointing to a thicket of tall bamboo in the distance. Before Felix could respond, an expected and uncomfortably familiar voice sounded behind them.

"A Chinese garden is more than a grouping of plants," Dr. Zhang said as he came into view, his long blue robes shimmering in the sunshine. "Please allow me to show you around." He greeted Felix with a subtle bow of his head, then introduced himself and Ming Su to Nichole. Finally, he tipped his head toward the figure at his elbow with a private smile. "I assume you have already met Felix's sister."

Melinda thrust out her hand in greeting. "When I told Dr. Zhang that you and Felix were going to be here today, he said you could join us." Her eyes narrowed as she tried to look through the dark lenses of Nichole's sunglasses.

Nichole shook Melinda's hand and bowed her head to Ming Su and Dr. Zhang. "*Nín hǎo*," she said in perfect Mandarin, then "I am very pleased to meet you" in French before switching to English. "Thank you for your kind offer. I don't think Felix will mind being replaced as my guide."

Dr. Zhang bowed his head again and swept out his arm toward the nearest bridges. "A Chinese garden focuses on the interdependence of the Earth's resources, showing the vibrancy that creates all life and energy on the planet." They walked onto the bridge, stopping in the middle and looking around as Dr. Zhang continued. "Water represents the principal of life; rocks, the bones of the earth. The plants are used for their beauty and symbolism. Everything has an integral role, just as it does in nature."

After an hour of slowly shuffling after Dr. Zhang and trying to look interested in his lengthy explanations, Felix was finding it increasingly difficult to stifle his yawns. Nichole didn't seem to notice: she gave Dr. Zhang her undivided attention, just as she would any teacher. She smiled at the right time, she frowned when appropriate, and she even looked genuinely amazed when he told her a story that was meant to…well…amaze her.

Melinda was also losing her interest in both the lecture and Nichole, who had not removed her dark sunglasses, giving her not even a glimpse of her eyes. As time dragged on, Melinda and Ming Su lagged farther and farther behind, stopping at the water's edge to admire the large golden carp that swam close to the surface or resting on a bench in a pavilion while Ming Su recited passages from *The Dreams of Min Min.*

Felix was looking back at his sister, envious and annoyed with her for getting him into this, when the sound of crackling explosions erupted near the entrance to the Garden.

"The dragon has arrived," Dr. Zhang announced. "Firecrackers are used to frighten away the evil spirits." Dr. Zhang led Nichole and Felix to the pavilion where Melinda and Ming Su were already watching the spectacle, peering through the milky cloud of smoke at several young men in blue and golden silken pajamas who paraded into the courtyard beating drums and clanging cymbals, announcing the arrival of the huge red dragon. Six men supported the dragon costume, dancing, leaping, dipping, and plunging as one, while the man at the head thrust it up and down, giving it a fearsome and powerful look as its eyes spun and its tongue lolled from side to side.

After the dragon dance, they were served tea, entertained by a strolling musician and then by other dancers, whose performance ended about the same time the sun had slipped below the tallest building, casting long shadows across the garden.

"I must be getting home now," Nichole said, removing her dark glasses at last and flashing a satisfied smile. "Thank you, Dr. Zhang, for the tour; I will always remember everything that you so kindly showed me this afternoon. And thank you for bringing me, Felix. I can't tell you when I've enjoyed myself more." She then turned toward Melinda, meeting her eyes for the first time. "And thank you, too, Melinda—because if it wasn't for you, your brother never would have brought me along."

Melinda stared unblinkingly into Nichole's eyes with a preoccupied expression. "That's okay. I'm…ah…glad you had a good time."

Dr. Zhang took Ming Su by the hand. "We too must be off. I have enjoyed sharing this time with all of you. Where we are from, we value the energy of the Earth; it is what makes all things possible." He bowed his head and smiled. "Come, Ming Su. We don't have much time."

As they turned to leave, Ming Su turned to face Melinda, meeting her eyes with a smile. "*Níg-ge-na-da a-ba in-da-di nam-ti ì-ù-tu.*"

CHAPTER TWENTY-SIX

Melinda stared after Ming Su and Dr. Zhang as they hurried through the gate. "Did you hear what she said?" she asked in a whisper, but Felix was already on his way to the exit, walking briskly toward the bus stop. "It's not her!" she called after him.

Felix looked at his watch. "The bus will be here any second, and if we don't catch this one we'll have to wait an hour for the next."

Melinda ran to catch him, grabbed his arm in an attempt to get him to listen to her. "Nichole isn't Indigo!"

"I take it you didn't see the ghosts," Felix said calmly, "which proves nothing. Isn't it possible you wouldn't see those images in their eyes all the time? I don't think that Stumpworthy always saw them." He tugged his arm away and walked a little faster. "She *is* Indigo—she speaks Mandarin, and for God's sake, she speaks Swahili."

"That doesn't prove anything. And besides, Indigo wasn't the one who spoke Swahili."

"We don't really know that, do we?"

They reached the bus stop just as the bus pulled up. "There's something else," Melinda whispered, eyeing the other passengers suspiciously. "I'll tell you about it when we get home— then maybe you'll understand."

Lights flickered on in shops and houses as the bus negotiated the long and silent journey home. By the time it pulled to a stop near the mansion, it was completely dark. The warmth of the day's sunshine gave way to a bitingly cold evening, making the walk from the bus stop and up the driveway a bitter experience. Felix and Melinda pulled their lightweight jackets tightly around themselves as they jogged up the steps and into the house, heading straight for the warm golden glow coming from the library. They found Professor Mulligan camped in his favorite chair, snorting and snoring peacefully while they scrambled to warm themselves in front of the crackling fire.

"Indigo isn't Nichole," Melinda started again, rubbing her hands together, "because Ming Su is."

Felix immediately forgot about being chilled to the bone. "You saw the ghosts in *her* eyes," Felix whispered back, to which Melinda nodded. "Isn't it possible she's just another traveler?"

"I don't know what all the possibilities are, but I do know that Nichole is as human as him," she said, jerking her head toward Mulligan. "It's like Dr. Zhang said: the eyes are the windows to the soul, and I am one of the few that can see inside a person's soul." Sensing Felix's confusion and stubbornness rising, she held up a hand. "Ming Su's eyes have exactly the same reflections that Indigo's had—*exactly*!

And if that isn't enough, she said this strange thing—the same thing Indigo said in my dream." Melinda closed her eyes, then whispered, *"Níg-ge-na-da a-ba in-da-di nam-ti ì-ù-tú"* in a voice that could have been Indigo's.

Felix nervously fiddled with his glasses as he asked in a high-pitched squeak, "How did you do that?"

"I don't know." Melinda smiled excitedly. "I went back in my memory and found the dream. I could see everything just as it had been the first time, like I was dreaming again. I saw Indigo at the white house and I heard her perfectly."

"You didn't change," Felix gasped. "Just your voice— you sounded just like her. Have you ever done this before?"

Melinda shook her head, then smiled slyly and closed her eyes, took a deep breath, and emitted the most bovine-like moo Felix had ever heard coming out of a non-cow. Her eyes popped open and she stared down at her hands, then peered in her reflection in the mirror that hung above the mantel, her expression transforming into a tremendous grin. "I'm not a cow, but I sounded just like one, didn't I?" She didn't wait for Felix's confirmation, continuing in a slightly louder voice, "I didn't know I could do this—it's got to be one of the coolest things that I've ever done."

Felix looked over at Professor Mulligan, who seemed undisturbed by Melinda's barnyard impression. "What was that thing you said before, the thing in Indigo's voice?"

"It's the same thing Ming Su said when she left the garden: *Níg-ge-na-da a-ba in-da-di nam-ti ì-ù-tu*."

"For some reason it sounds familiar," Felix said absently. He paused, tapping his temple for a second before whipping his head around to stare at his sister. "Now I remember; I was talking to Indigo about some proverb you'd told me— something about feet…"

"Binding your feet to prevent your own progress?"

"Yeah, that was it. And when she left, she said that thing. It's probably some kind of Chinese proverb, too."

Professor Mulligan snorted, his eyes fluttering open as he interrupted with a disgustingly raspy clearing of his throat, "That is not Chinese; it is ancient Sumerian." He answered their astonished stares with a pleased nod. "I took a course in ancient languages at university, and we did a small unit on Sumerian, mainly focusing on popular sayings. I remember it well. I had to chant that phrase over and over and over to remember it for an exam—big waste of time, if you ask me. *Níg-ge-na-da a-ba in-da-di nam-ti ì-ù-tu*. Whoever has walked with truth generates life."

Felix eyed him suspiciously. "Are you sure you remember correctly? Weren't you at university a long time ago?"

"My boy," Mulligan chuckled, "it was indeed a *long* time ago, but I can assure you I remember it as if I learnt it only yesterday, just as I would a poem or a song."

"I don't get it. Why would Indigo and Ming Su be reciting some weird Sumerian saying?"

Melinda touched his shoulder. "I just told you; they're the same person."

Felix massaged the bridge of his nose and shook his head. "How is any of this possible? Why did Indigo become a little Chinese girl? And what does a Sumerian saying have to do with anything?"

Melinda looked down at her feet and shook her head. "It's definitely not like the stories."

"It's not like anything! First we thought Indigo had some kind of relationship with the dead, like a medium. Then we thought she was a time traveler like those stories." Felix looked at James Mulligan for answers, only to see the tiny dribbles of saliva oozing out of the comers of his mouth, signaling that the professor was dozing again. He sighed. "I just wish we knew what she is, where she's going, and why."

Melinda nodded. "I guess my idea about Athenites being the guides was wrong. If Ming Su has any guide, it's definitely Dr. Zhang. Did Indigo have anyone?"

"The only person I ever heard her talk about was her Aunt Phoebe, but she didn't say much about her." Felix looked out across the room without seeing the bookshelves or the windows, not focusing on anything in particular. "'Whoever has walked with truth generates life.' What do you think it means?" Melinda searched her mind for a plausible explanation, but in the end it was Felix who snapped his fingers. "*Knowledge*," he said excitedly. "It must have something to do with truth in knowledge."

Melinda frowned. "I don't get it."

Felix was becoming more agitated, and stood up to pace in front of the hearth. "They travel to gain knowledge, which allows them to travel to gain more knowledge, thereby giving them life. Which could explain why they change shape." When he noticed the confused puppy look on Melinda's face, he patted her on the head and smiled. "Don't you see? To truly gain knowledge, you must be able to see the world through others' eyes—what better way to do that than by becoming other people?"

"I get it now." Melinda nodded seriously. "So they keep traveling until they have all the knowledge they need, then they leave. I wonder if that's why Courtney died."

Felix looked like all the happiness had drained out of him as his shoulders dropped. "When they have all the knowledge they need, they leave," he repeated morosely.

For the next few minutes, the popping sounds of burning wood mixed with the occasional sputtering wheezes from the professor were the only sounds in the library. Felix paced quietly with his hands clasped behind his back, his head down as he stared at a spot always just in front of his feet.

"Felix," Melinda said softly, "when Dr. Zhang and Ming Su left the garden, he said they had to hurry: that they didn't have much time. Do you think they're already gone?"

Felix's complexion turned ashen. "I hope not," he said softly. "I can't lose her again—not without saying goodbye."

CHAPTER TWENTY-SEVEN

Whoever has walked with truth generates life rang in Felix's mind as he stared at the red C his teacher had marked on his quiz paper, followed by *Not your best work Mr. Hutton.*

"So what are you thinking about when you should be thinking about quantum physics?" Nichole asked as she passed his desk.

Felix slipped the paper into his folder and stood up slowly. "Nothing important—just something my sister said," he mumbled as he gathered his books and then held out his arm to motion her to go first.

"I don't mean to pry, but you look concerned about something. Is everything all right?" she asked as they left the classroom.

Felix deliberately dodged the question, looking instead his watch. "It's lunchtime…do you want to get something to eat?"

Felix found a table in the crowded cafeteria while Nichole went to get her lunch, then waited patiently while he went to get his. By the time they both sat down to eat, the lunch period was almost over.

"You didn't answer my question earlier. Is something going on with you?" Nichole asked just as Felix stuffed a large portion of his sandwich into his mouth. His mouth so full he could hardly chew, let alone speak, Felix shrugged, hoping that that would satisfy her. Nichole folded her arms and leaned forward across the table. "I want to know what's bothering you."

Felix eyed her reluctantly, swallowing the last bits of bread. "Nothing's bothering me. I'm just having trouble concentrating on my schoolwork today."

"That's impossible," she laughed. "Your superior concentration with regard to your studies is legendary."

"Well, right now I'm afraid it's not *superior*, it's not even adequate," he said with disdain.

"You can tell me what's bothering you if you want. I won't judge or meddle. Just, sometimes it's nice to share troubles with someone else, making the weight of your problem seem a little lighter."

Felix looked at her as if seeing her again for the first time, realizing he really didn't know her at all, having imagined her as Indigo for so long. Maybe she was right, he decided; at least he could talk about the one thing that was bothering him most.

"It's really complicated, but I keep thinking about this saying: *whoever has walked with truth generates life.*"

Nichole smiled as if recalling a wonderful secret. "That's Babylonian, isn't it?" She laughed, noticing the startled look on Felix's face. "Don't look so surprised…you're not the only one to have heard that saying. My grandmother told me the story when I was only five and I still remember every word—it was my favorite. I can't believe you aren't able to concentrate because you're thinking about a children's story about a camel."

"A camel," Felix asked incredulously.

Nichole nodded. "A camel, an elephant, and a lion to be exact," she said, "and the moral was that whoever walks with truth generates life…very deep stuff for a five-year-old."

Elaine Hutton greeted Dr. Zhang at the front door. "I must compliment you on your teaching style; I have never seen Melinda so engaged in her studies. Hardly a day goes by that she doesn't talk about Chinese history."

Dr. Zhang smiled. "She is a bright student, one with great insight and understanding. I have enjoyed my time with her."

"She'll be upset when she learns you are no longer able to teach her."

They walked down the hallway in silence, but just before reaching the library, Dr. Zhang stopped and looked at Elaine. "Melinda will do very well in all her studies because she has learnt how to gather knowledge, how to question the things she is told and accept the things that she understands; she has learned the fine art of truly being a student. It will serve her well on her journey."

He bowed low and then stepped into the library, leaving Elaine behind with a confused look on her face.

"Ah, Melinda," he greeted with a bow of his head.

Melinda bowed in kind. "I was thinking you might not be here today."

Dr. Zhang nodded. "You are as perceptive as I have grown to expect." He crossed the room and took his usual seat. "In that case, what I have to say won't be too much of a surprise: this will be our last lesson."

"Are you and Ming Su going away?" she asked, looking into eyes that, for once, he didn't try to hide from her.

Dr. Zhang looked down at his hands for several seconds before raising his head with a smile. "We have finished what we have come here to do."

Melinda took a deep breath as her eyes filled with tears. "Is your journey finished? Will I ever see you again?"

Dr. Zhang looked momentarily anxious before returning to his normal calm demeanor. "I must remember what you are capable of understanding." He glanced briefly away before locking gazes with Melinda again. "In my travels, I have met many like you, and I often forget about your special talents of recognition." His expression had an intensity Melinda had never seen before. "In all my travels I have been careful to remain mysterious, never trusting even those with whom I am charged—it is difficult even for them to understand. I sense from you that you must live with the same secrecy; you and I are similar in that way. I think it's time we learn to be honest with one another. We know more about each other than we are willing to say."

Melinda closed her eyes as she tried to penetrate his thoughts, but it was like looking into a black hole where nothing existed. Nervously she opened her eyes and saw his gaze still fixed on her.

"May I ask you a question?" she finally managed in a voice just above a whisper.

"You may ask anything you wish."

The problem was that Melinda didn't know what to ask. She looked down at her hands, then stared straight ahead for several seconds before taking a deep breath, speaking rapidly as if she didn't want him to hear her. "Are you the guide?"

Dr. Zhang folded his hands calmly in his lap. "Yes, I suppose I am."

Melinda couldn't believe what she was hearing and could barely contain her excitement. She was sitting opposite the guide himself, the person who took others on fantastic voyages through time. "At first I thought Felix was." She giggled, then her expression became serious again. "In the stories, animals seemed important, so I figured they were like us. I thought we were the important ones."

"You are important; you are a fellow traveler who connects with us because you can recognize us. Animals and those with animal senses have that ability, but humans do not."

Melinda nodded. "Why do you have to go?"

Dr. Zhang didn't answer immediately, as if he hadn't wanted to. "Our journey is complete."

"I don't understand."

Dr. Zhang smiled kindly. "A person's journey belongs only to them, and no others need to understand. Most people do not understand their own destiny; Ming Su does not know her future, just as you do not know yours. But with every soul, each individual influences their future through the knowledge they have gathered in their life on Earth. There is a proverb…*qian shi bu wang, hou shi zhi shi*: use incidents from the past as lessons for the future. Many people think they live their lives according to this proverb, but in reality very few can. Only when a person has accomplished this can their time on Earth be complete."

Melinda wasn't sure that she understood completely, but she nodded anyway. "Where are you going?"

He stared at her with even more intensity than before, unlocking his thoughts for her to see and understand. "We are going to the place where we are destined to be."

Felix arranged his books around one of the computers in the school's library, opened his chemistry book to the assigned chapters on *Aqueous Solutions and Solubility Equilibria,* then refocused on the computer screen as he logged onto the system. A search page illuminated the monitor. Without a second look at his book or a second thought about what he needed to do, he began typing:

Camel + Elephant + Lion + Babylon + Sumerian

In seconds the first ten out of 12,000 items were displayed. Felix scanned the entries about zoos in Iraq, zoos in the Middle East, zoos with the best African and Asian animals, and zoos of ancient times until he came to the 160th entry: ancient fables. The title read, *How the Camel gained the knowledge that helped the Lion and the Elephant.*

For the next fifteen minutes, Felix read the ancient story about a lion searching the Earth for truth with the elephant as his guide. Together they traveled through the jungles and talked to the animals. The monkey told them how it lived in the trees to stay safe from the panther. The panther told them how it roamed the forest and plains to find food for its young. The wild boar told of feasting on roots that other animals ignored. And the ant showed them its incredible underground fortress and introduced them to a million of its cousins.

One day, their journey took them to a large desert, where they met a camel. The camel warned them not to cross the desert, for surely they would die, as there was no water for more than ten days' walk. The camel shared all his knowledge about the desert, telling them of the oasis with its date palm trees laden with fruit, of the winds that lifted the sand and threw it in all directions, making it impossible to see. When the camel had shared all its knowledge with them, they knew the time had come for their journey's end.

"We have walked with truth all our lives and possess all the knowledge of the world. It is now time for us to leave this place," the lion said to the elephant.

The camel looked at them and sighed. "I too have all the knowledge that I can hold," to which the lion replied, "I can see that in your eyes, and I know you are to travel with us. Our lives here are complete. Death awaits us so that we may explore the heavens as we have been destined to do."

CHAPTER TWENTY-EIGHT

Melinda sat on the bottom step of the staircase in the foyer, staring at the front door with an unwavering gaze. She seemed to look right through Felix when he walked in and stood for a moment in the doorway, his original destination of the library temporarily forgotten.

"They're not coming back," she whispered, so softly Felix wasn't sure if he was meant to hear her or not.

He studied his sister's zombie-like pose. "Who's not coming back?"

"Dr. Zhang and Ming Su," she answered.

"Is this another one of your dreams?"

Melinda shook her head solemnly. "He was here today. He *is* a time traveler—he *is* the guide."

Felix frowned, thinking Melinda seemed unusually somber for having such exciting news. He shrugged it off as another of his sister's weird moods and jerked his head toward the hallway with a smile. "These books are really heavy; come down to the library and you can tell me what's going on." He didn't wait for her to reply before turning and walking away.

It wasn't until he disappeared from view that Melinda slowly got to her feet and shuffled after him. She arrived in the library completely dazed, not really remembering how she got there or why she had come. She made her way to the center sofa, sat down, and then looked at her hands as if seeing them for the first time.

"He knows I can read his mind and he knows I can recognize people like him," she announced. "He told me he has met people like us before." She rested her head on the back of the sofa and stared up at nothing. "He told me about destiny, and how when a person completes things here, when they have achieved *qian shi bu wang, hou shi zhi shi*, they leave Earth."

Felix looked up with a frown. "I don't know what you're talking about."

"It's a proverb: Use incidents from the past as lessons for the future."

Felix rolled his eyes and took a deep breath, fighting the urge to harass her about yet another proverb. "Of course—learn from the past, because history has a way of repeating itself," he offered, pushing his sliding glasses into place. "True knowledge takes that into account. People with knowledge don't make the same mistakes over and over. They learn from their mistakes and move on."

Melinda nodded. "So when they finally learn all there is to learn, they leave for good."

Felix felt a strange panicky feeling welling up in his chest.

"Did he tell you how they leave or where they end up?"

Melinda closed her eyes and recalled Dr. Zhang's voice in her mind. *"Our journey is complete. We are going to the place that we are destined to be."*

Felix's face drained of color as he stared at his sister. Images of the camel leaving with the lion and elephant to explore the heavens mixed with images of the high priestess in *Harrani* and Min Min leaving the world. In the stories, the characters left for something better, but the result in reality could only mean one thing—the same thing that had happened to Courtney. "Did he suggest he was about to die?"

"He didn't use the word, but I think that's what he meant."

Felix shook his head to chase away the image of Dr. Zhang and Ming Su being struck by a bus.

Melinda turned to face him, her eyes glassy. "Right after that, I looked into his eyes. I saw Indigo. She was smiling and looked really happy, as if she was excited about something. Then I saw Ming Su. She looked happy too. She was holding someone's hand." A single tear rolled down Melinda's cheek as she took a deep breath. "I couldn't see the person clearly at first, but then I did. It was me—I was walking with her."

"You're not one of them," Felix barked desperately. "You can't go with them!"

Melinda shook her head. "He said I was important; he said I was a traveler too." She looked over at the grandfather clock, its pendulum swinging slowly as if it were driving the time instead of simply keeping track of it. Two tears slowly trickled down her face. "I always want time to speed by," she said softly. "Now I wish it would just stop." She looked over at Felix, who stood frozen in front of the hearth. "I'm not ready to go—I still make the same mistakes over and over, and I haven't learned everything yet."

Felix looked up thoughtfully and nodded. "They must not be big enough mistakes."

Melinda looked defeated. "I used to think time travel would be fun, like taking a holiday. I would daydream about visiting Marie Antoinette and having tea. I thought it would be like in the movies, when time travelers amazed people with things from the future and were treated like gods. But I don't think it's like that."

"Apparently not," Felix responded, feeling numb. "Look—Mum's picking Dad up from the airport right now. They'll be home soon, and they'll know what to do. Maybe I should call Harmony and Mulligan. Have you been in touch with Joe?"

Melinda shook her head slowly. "He's been really busy; I can't break into his thoughts." She stood up and walked across to the fireplace, staring into the cold hearth. "Wait a minute," she blurted out. "I could transform—that way they'd never find me." She didn't wait for a response from Felix before she closed her eyes, and within an instant was gone.

Felix stared at Melinda's clothes in a heap on the floor for several seconds before gingerly lifting first her shirt, then her trousers. A small gray mouse with Melinda's freckled face stared up at him. He picked her up, holding her in his palm as he analyzed the tiny details of her transformation. Her paws, fur, and tail were all flawless; everything except the face was mouse-like perfection. "Invisibility would probably be more effective," he mused, more to himself than to her.

"That *would* be a neat trick," said a strange, translucent boy standing in the doorway, causing Felix to squeeze Melinda in his fist as he stumbled backward.

"How did you get in here?" Felix shouted, unable to control the quiver in his voice as he stared at the semi-transparent aberration addressing him. He was taller than Felix by only a few centimeters, with the same slim build; his hair was ginger and his face was strong and handsome, as if chiseled out of stone. It was also completely see-through. Because his clothes were transparent as well, Felix knew he must be talking to a ghost.

The boy stepped into the library, locking eyes with Felix. "I hadn't realized you cannot see me as Melinda does."

"I can see you," Felix snapped, trying to remember if Melinda had ever mentioned any friendship with a ghost. He inched backward as the boy walked toward him. "What are you…who are you?"

Another voice resonated from behind the boy, a familiar voice Felix couldn't believe he was hearing. "I know this is very confusing for you," Indigo soothed, coming into view as she stepped up next to the boy. She had the same ghostly pallor, the same translucent form. "It was for me too, but I have learned to accept the thing that I cannot change, and now I look forward to my next adventure, just as we all learn to do."

Part
Three

CHAPTER TWENTY-NINE

Indigo glided over to Felix, placing her hand over the one that held Melinda. Her touch was cool and soft, like a whisper of breath that went through the back of his hand and into his palm. He jerked away, clutching Melinda a little tighter, and then wishing that he hadn't, panicking when he realized he couldn't feel her movements or the thumping of her tiny heart. He trembled, wondering if she was all right but too afraid to open his hand to check.

Melinda held perfectly still, partly due to the pressure of Felix's hand, partly out of fear, but mostly so she could hear what was being said, which wasn't much. The thickness of Felix's fingers muffled what would otherwise have been booming voices. Then all of a sudden a strange cool sensation penetrated her entire body and Felix clutched her tighter.

"You might hurt her, holding her like that," Indigo scolded as she looked down at Felix's hand.

Felix backed up until he bumped into the corner of a sofa. "What are you doing here?" was all he could think to say.

"It is time for us to leave," Indigo answered, with a look on her face that suggested Felix should have known that.

Felix looked at Indigo and held up his free hand in a wave. "Bye, then."

Indigo gave him a sideways glance. "Felix," she began, then shook her head. "Not without…" She paused and looked pleadingly at her companion. "He doesn't know?"

The boy didn't answer, holding out his hand to Felix. "I want Melinda to experience this."

"NO!" Felix yelled, trying to get around the sofa—to exactly where, he didn't know.

Indigo shook her head and closed her eyes. "Felix, it's not supposed to be like this. We were meant to leave after we, ah…" She stopped herself, giving the boy a worried look.

"After we died," he finished for her.

Felix felt dizzy. His legs wouldn't hold him anymore, and he collapsed onto the sofa, his hands trembling in his lap. He looked up at the smiling Indigo. "When…how…" he stammered, then shook his head. "I'm sorry."

"Don't worry, I won't take offense." Indigo laughed. "Actually, it was all rather interesting. I had never died before."

The boy shook his head. "Not that you would recall. You don't remember the other times, and you shouldn't have known about this time. Nobody ever remembers—they just go on to the next step, the next journey as if it were the only one they would ever experience. It's the way it's supposed to be. I'm beginning to think it was a mistake to let you know any of this, but you are, after all, a special case."

Felix stared at the ghostly forms conversing in front of him, thinking he would love to dissolve into invisibility himself when the tiny prick of Melinda's nails against his hand reminded him why he couldn't. He had to find a way to protect her, to prevent them from doing whatever they planned to do.

Indigo gave Felix the sweetest smile he had ever seen. "Can we see Melinda now? We really do have to go."

Felix noticed both Indigo and the boy were becoming more transparent as the seconds ticked away. His mind raced with the thought that if he simply stalled long enough they wouldn't be able to take her. "I won't let you do this," he snarled, wrapping his other hand over the knot that held Melinda.

The boy shook his head. "You don't understand," he said. "Nothing can prevent destiny. Death will come when it's meant to arrive—you must not hurry it along or fight against it. Your eternal journey will only continue when it's destined to."

Felix felt a sickness in the pit of his stomach, wondering if Melinda would simply vanish from his hand. "Why Melinda...why does it have to be her?" he pleaded, turning back to Indigo.

Indigo looked at her companion, her expression making it clear she didn't know the answer. The boy smiled back at her. "She has many talents that must be looked upon as gifts. I told her before that I've met others with similar talents in my travels, but none with such intuitiveness and open-mindedness. Her innocence allows her to be truly honest in a way that others cannot understand."

Felix looked down at his hands, clenched together to protect his sister. Thoughts rushed through his mind about their lives together—her annoying habits, her giddy willingness to transform into anything, the spark of excitement she brought to their family. The boy was right; she *was* special. She had gifts Felix had to admit he admired and often envied. He opened his hands to reveal the little mouse body of Melinda, her eyes squinting against the bright light as she looked up at him and then over at Indigo and the boy.

"Dr. Zhang," she said in a tiny voice that matched her size.

The boy nodded and smiled. "You are truly amazing," he said as he held his hand out toward her. She climbed onto his palm, never taking her eyes from his. Several seconds passed with the two locked in a mutual stare. "Thank you," the boy finally whispered. "You have given me a special gift on my last journey home." He then placed her gently on the floor next to him.

Indigo looked over at Felix; tears that had been massing were beginning to trickle down his cheeks. "Please don't be sad. I hope that in some way I am allowed to remember our friendship. You are a very special person, Felix Hutton." She looked over at her companion and smiled. "Adam, I'm ready."

Felix stared into Indigo's eyes as she began fading, evaporating into nothingness. He glanced briefly at the boy she had called Adam to see that he was almost gone too; only a faint outline remained as he smiled and nodded in parting. It was like watching steam evaporate into clear air until nothing remained of them. Felix dropped his head forward as he covered his face with his hands, unable to prevent the deluge of tears from cascading onto his glasses, overflowing and then dribbling through his fingers as he rocked back and forth. He couldn't bring himself to look at the last spot where Melinda had stood.

CHAPTER THIRTY

The sound of Felix's sobs and the ticking of the clock seemed absorbed into a black hole of silence as the library took on a surreal stillness. Felix didn't know how much time had elapsed—a few minutes? A few hours?

Without opening his eyes, he leaned back against the sofa, letting his head rest a few seconds before removing his glasses. He dropped them onto his lap, then massaged his eyes, which were now swollen and sore. At last he looked up, trying to focus his blurred vision on the domed ceiling three stories above him before braving a glance at the place where Melinda had been.

He straightened immediately when he saw her, standing in the same place. It was Melinda's image, he was certain of that, but she lacked any kind of identifying detail. All her features seemed blended together, only differentiated by darker and lighter areas; he could make out the blue of her eyes but not their shape, and all her freckles seemed to meld together, making her face look like a beige blob.

He fumbled to get his glasses back on in hopes that the picture would clear, but it didn't. The ghostly images of Indigo and Adam were gone, but for some reason Melinda was still there.

"Felix," she said softly, "are you going to be all right?"

Felix's eyes widened as he realized she must have stayed behind to make sure he was okay. "I don't know…this is all so impossible."

"I know it is, but I suppose we should have expected it."

Felix shook his head. "If there was only something I could have done—if only Mum and Dad had been here, or Joe, or Harmony…"

"They couldn't have done anything to prevent this either. It's destiny."

Felix didn't answer immediately, mulling over what exactly he could say, how he could understand what was happening, how to help ease the pain. "Why did they choose you?"

"I'm special," she said in a teasing way. "I've been telling you that for years."

"You almost sound happy about this." His tone had become harsh.

"I am," she replied. "You would have been, too! Are you jealous because it was me and not you?"

"I cannot believe you think I would be jealous of…of… of death!" He regretting saying it, but there was no taking it back.

Melinda leaned forward, then started to laugh. "You really should practice your mind reading." She tore Felix's glasses off his face and rubbed them on her shirt. "These are filthy! You must have cried a whole bucket of tears on these lenses—let alone all those greasy finger prints! There," she said, handing them back to him. "Now take a look."

Felix's hands were shaking as he readjusted his glasses to sit on the bridge of his nose. "You're not a ghost," he said in amazement.

Now giggling almost uncontrollably, Melinda shook her head. "I know how to read minds."

"That's how you got away? You read their minds?" Felix felt giddy but confused.

"I was never meant to go with them. Adam only wanted to share things with me that he had never been able to tell anyone before. He said this was his last journey and he had always wanted to tell someone about his life, but no one would have believed him. He thought I would understand because I feel the same way, wishing I could tell everyone I'm an Athenite. He trusted me, so he opened his mind to me."

Felix rocked back against the sofa. "You're still alive," he said through an exhale. "But Indigo and Adam are…"

"Gone," she finished for him. "They have left for their next journey, only this time it won't be on Earth." She crossed over and sat next to him, wrapping her arm around his shoulders. "They were born on Earth and traveled for centuries, gaining knowledge to help them become the people they needed to be to fulfill their destiny. Their time on Earth is over. Adam wasn't sad; neither was Indigo. In fact, they said they were excited to go on to their next adventure."

"Did they choose to go?"

Melinda shook her head. "They have to travel along the path they are destined to follow. They must live naturally and die when it's their time to go; they must make the most of what they are given. It really is like the stories about Delondra and Min Min—they must have been written to help people understand." She paused and looked out across the room. "Adam said every life is an adventure. Sometimes they are long and sometimes short, but that doesn't matter in the greater scheme of things."

Felix looked at her, finally managing a smile. "Are they off to that island?"

"Paradise Shore." Melinda smiled back. "I don't know, but I do know that wherever they've gone is wonderful. It's where they want to be, doing exactly what they want to do. He said that when they are born in this new place, they'll know exactly how they want to live after all their travels on Earth." She rested her head on the back of the sofa and looked up at the ceiling. "He let me see a city park where they were going. It had a row of trees through the middle and flowers blooming neatly along a path. The sun was shining and there were lots of people about, riding bikes and rollerblading. A whole bunch of people, it might have been a hundred or more, were playing a game on the grass—they would run one way and then the other, all chasing this strange ball. I don't know how to explain the feeling that I had, except to say that I knew everyone was happy, and completely satisfied. I don't think you could be sad to go, if that's where you were going."

CHAPTER THIRTY-ONE

Mia stared at the swirling colors of *Renewal* and smiled. She took a deep, satisfying breath as she smoothed her silky black hair away from her face. "Thank you," she said softly. "That was amazing—reliving my history, knowing where I've come from. Will I always remember those experiences?"

Adam looked over his shoulder and nodded at Anya Harding, who was standing with Alfred Canat at the back of the room. "You'll remember everything...and nothing."

Mia's eyes narrowed as she tried to understand. She turned away from the painting, looking at Adam as if seeing him for the first time. "Your hair has changed, hasn't it? It's blonde now. Wasn't it red before?"

"I look more like my family now," he answered with a shrug, "just like you look like yours. You look a lot like you did when you were Indigo."

Mia looked at the soft bronze color of her skin. "I've been traveling for centuries; how much time has passed here?"

Adam looked at Anya again, as if for guidance. Anya lowered her eyes, looping her arm through Alfred Canat's as they walked slowly out of the gallery. Adam turned his attention back to Mia and smiled. "We've been gone about an hour."

Mia looked at the painting once more. "I understand the images now," she said, letting her gaze take in the other paintings that lined the walls of the gallery. "I recognize it because I was there—they are all images of the Earth, aren't they?"

Adam smiled and nodded. "It's where we began, where we were born and then reborn. Every Servalian has experienced the first part of their journey there, where we gained the knowledge and wisdom to allow us to come here."

Mia looked quizzically at Adam and grimaced. "So Servalius is the end for us?"

Adam shrugged. "I don't know, but I wouldn't think so. People die here, too. I can only imagine where their next journey will take them."

Mia looked around at the brilliant images adorning the walls. A warm feeling spread throughout her body, a feeling of happiness—of homecoming. "They're all so fantastic—so beautiful."

Adam nodded. "They are the reflections of the one thing we cannot exist without, images of our mother and father and reason for being: the Earth. Our world cannot exist without its ever-changing renewal and energy."

Mia looked at him. "The Earth never stops changing, does it?"

"It changes with or without us," he said with pride.

Mia looked sad for only an instant. "But we stay the same."

"If by that you mean humans are humans regardless of the age in which they live, with the same basic desires and instincts, then I agree with you. But we do change as individuals through the knowledge we collect."

"Does everyone go back like you and I did?"

"No. Through some strange accident, you arrived here too early—you experienced an accidental death that was not meant to happen. From what I understand, it happens from time to time. So you had to return to finish your journey— to gather the knowledge that would help you understand who you were to become. Something similar happened to me, but instead of repeating the things I was meant to do in the first place, I was made your guide."

Mia giggled for the first time. "You were my cat, weren't you?"

Adam's cheeks reddened. "And your aunt Phoebe and an old Chinese man, as well as a lot of other things."

Mia's eyes twinkled in the sunshine that lit the room. "You said I would remember nothing and everything."

"Your knowledge is what makes you who you are, so that will remain, but your understanding about how you gathered it will fade. Your knowledge of Earth will also fade away, but you will always celebrate the images you see in this gallery. They are the windows that connect us."

An amazed expression overtook Mia's face. "Who *is* Anya?"

"She is the artist who brings the images to us. For generations, her family have been the guardians of the reason for our being—our history."

Mia wasn't sure she understood, but she didn't press for more details. "Since you were my guide, does that mean you'll go back?"

Adam shook his head. "My journey there is finally complete—thanks to you. Now I can go forward, just like every other Servalian." He looked into her eyes and saw the question she wanted to ask. "No," he answered before she could say a word. "I will be just like you; I won't remember."

They stepped down from the stage and walked slowly out of the gallery into the warm sunshine. People were still enjoying their day; Baffleball was in full swing in the park, and children and adults sped by on bicycles and rollerblades. Mia smiled, but there was sadness in her eyes.

"I wish I was allowed to remember some things."

Adam shook his head. "That would lead to dwelling on your past experiences. We are all meant to live in the present and look toward the future." Adam saw the disappointment on her face and raised an eyebrow before nudging her in the ribs. "You want to remember Felix Hutton, don't you?"

Two crimson dots burnt on Mia's cheeks. "He was a good friend—just like you." They walked a little farther in silence. "Will he remember us? Will Melinda?"

Adam shrugged. "I don't know where their destiny will take them or what they will remember along the way. We may meet them again in another place, in another time. The next journey is as mysterious to them as it is to us. Destiny has a way of sorting these things out. Our job is simply to follow our own path."

At last Mia gave into a smile. Her thoughts of her other lives were already fading, the memories of the painting becoming a pleasant haze in her mind. Before she forgot, she spared one last thought of gratitude for the friends they had left behind—then she slipped her hand into Adam's and gave in to the brilliance of the setting sun, content to find out where this path led side by side.

ACKNOWLEDGMENTS

The impetus for this book came from a photographic exhibit I visited at the Natural History Museum in London (UK). Thank you to the curators for your fascinating exhibits and dedication to the study of the natural history of our world providing an inspiration for all.

As always I owe a debt of gratitude to all the readers who helped me fine-tune this story and to my agent Fiona Spencer Thomas who has always been supportive and encouraging over the years. Thank you too to everyone at MP Publishing who believed in this project with special thanks to Mark, Alison, Joanne and Michelle for your energy and dedication in making this book a reality.

And a very big thank you to my wonderful family; I love you all!